"Mary, do you care about me enough to give me an off-to-work kiss?" Bruce asked.

His hazel-green eyes were dancing and filled with a warmth that she felt right into her bones. She tried to pull away from him, but his left hand was flat on the small of her back, his right still under her chin, caressing her throat. She wondered if he could feel the wild pulse there. "I couldn't do that. You might be late for work."

His grin was full of mischief. "What kind of kiss are you thinking about? A quick, off-to-work kiss wouldn't make me late. But if you have something else in mind, I'm willing to risk it."

'Um—oh—" She was embarrassed. Of course a quick kiss wouldn't make him late. The mesmerizing thought of even a brief embrace shared with him kept her enthralled. Then she noticed the dimple next to the left-hand corner of his mouth, and she wanted very badly to place her lips over it.

"Just a little kiss," he said softly, leaning closer so she could feel his breath on her cheek. Alarm bells clanged loudly in her head, but the growing hunger in his eyes, hunger she knew must be echoed in her own, filled her blood with a need she could no longer deny. Then his mouth brushed hers, and she was his. . . .

P9-AOY-639

WHAT ARE *LOVESWEPT* ROMANCES?

They are stories of true romance and touching emotion. We believe those two very important ingredients are constants in our highly sensual and very believable stories in the *LOVESWEPT* line. Our goal is to give you, the reader, stories of consistently high quality that may sometimes make you laugh, sometimes make you cry, but are always fresh and creative and contain many delightful surprises within their pages.

Most romance fans read an enormous number of books. Those they truly love, they keep. Others may be traded with friends and soon forgotten. We hope that each *LOVESWEPT* romance will be a treasure—a "keeper." We will always try to publish

LOVE STORIES YOU'LL NEVER FORGET
BY AUTHORS YOU'LL ALWAYS REMEMBER

The Editors

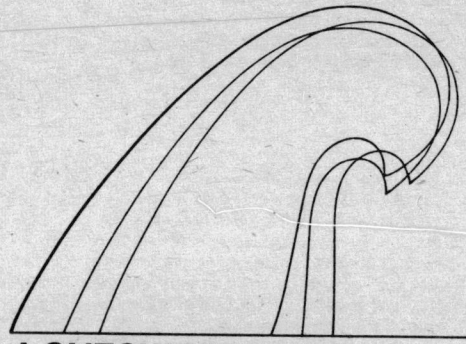

LOVESWEPT® • 406

Judy Gill
Desperado

BANTAM BOOKS
NEW YORK • TORONTO • LONDON • SYDNEY • AUCKLAND

DESPERADO

A Bantam Book / June 1990

*LOVESWEPT® and the wave device are registered
trademarks of Bantam Books, a division of
Bantam Doubleday Dell Publishing Group, Inc.
Registered in U.S. Patent
and Trademark Office and elsewhere.*

*All rights reserved.
Copyright © 1990 by Judy Gill.
Cover art copyright © 1990 by Hal Frenck.
No part of this book may be reproduced or transmitted
in any form or by any means, electronic or mechanical,
including photocopying, recording, or by any information
storage and retrieval system, without permission in
writing from the publisher.
For information address: Bantam Books.*

*If you would be interested in receiving protective vinyl
covers for your Loveswept books, please write to this address
for information:*

Loveswept
Bantam Books
P.O. Box 985
Hicksville, NY 11802

ISBN 0-553-44037-3

Published simultaneously in the United States and Canada

*Bantam Books are published by Bantam Books, a division
of Bantam Doubleday Dell Publishing Group, Inc. Its trademark, consisting of the words "Bantam Books" and the
portrayal of a rooster, is Registered in U.S. Patent and
Trademark Office and in other countries. Marca Registrada.
Bantam Books, 666 Fifth Avenue, New York, New York 10103.*

PRINTED IN THE UNITED STATES OF AMERICA

OPM   0 9 8 7 6 5 4 3 2 1

For Sean Nicholas
born July 5, 1989—destined to be a hero

One

"San-ta Lu-cia! Santa . . . Lucia!"

Mary rolled over in bed, pulled a pillow over her head, and groaned. Outside the racket continued. She glanced at her watch on her bedside table. It wasn't even eleven o'clock. She'd had less than two hours sleep. Who in the world was making that dreadful din? And why? Finally, she got up, tugged on a robe, rubbed her eyes, and stomped to the patio doors that led to her balcony. Sliding them open, she stepped out into the hot morning sun.

"Hark! How the sailors cry, joyous the echoes high . . ."

"Oh, my goodness!" Leaning over the rail of her third-story balcony, she gasped when she saw the man one suite over and one floor down, who was singing the raucous melody. She blinked in disbelief.

He lay partially in a child's wading pool, head and shoulders and much of his torso out the port side, leaning on the slide, hands behind his head, eyes shut tightly against the glare of the sun, legs from the knees down hanging out over the starboard side, straddling the frog's head.

She called out, "Uh—mister!" But he gave no sign of having heard her. He wore boldly patterned swim-

1

ming trunks, a black mustache with drooping ends that made him look like a desperado, a gold wristwatch that glinted in the sun, a set of headphones, and a superb tan on his superb body.

But Mary wasn't there to admire some stranger's body, she reminded herself. She was there to ensure some peace and quiet in the neighborhood so she could get a few hours of badly needed sleep. After all, that was the main reason she lived in this particular apartment complex. It was adults only, which meant that the other tenants were usually at work during the day when she needed to sleep. What this man was doing on his patio at eleven o'clock in the morning was beyond her. If he worked at night like she did, then why wasn't he sleeping? And if he worked during the day, why wasn't he doing so?

"Hey!" she shouted, and he responded by beginning another loud verse. She yelled again, with the same lack of result, and glanced around for something a little more obvious to attract his attention. Gritting her teeth, she picked up a vase of flowers from the table and flung its contents across and down. The water hit the man in the chest and splashed up into his face, breaking his song off in midphrase.

He lifted his head, shoulders, and torso. His legs snapped inward and folded until he sat in the water, tailor-fashion. He looked perplexed, and picked a flower off his chest, gazing at its sodden stem, its bent yellow petals. He wrinkled his nose and sneezed.

"Hey!" said Mary again, and he looked up at her, pulling down the headphones so they draped around his neck.

"Hey?" he repeated. "Hey, what? Hey, me?"

"Yes, dammit! Hey, you!"

"What's your problem, lady? Did you throw these things at me?" He plucked another flower off his flat belly and tossed it over the rail.

"Yes, I threw those things at you! I had to get your attention."

He sneezed again. "Well, you've got it. What is this? A new version of the Welcome Wagon?"

"No, it's a polite request to please be quiet. I was trying to sleep, and with that caterwauling going on, it's impossible."

"Caterwauling?" Abruptly, he stood in the middle of his pool, hands on hips, feet splayed apart, head tilted back, water clinging to and glinting in the dark, curling hair on his legs. "Caterwauling?" He drew in a deep breath, increasing the breadth of his chest by several inches, and let it out again in an explosive sneeze. "That . . . uh . . . uh . . . was sing . . . ing and I . . . I . . . Ah-choo! I . . . I . . . Ah-choo! Oh, Lord! Ah-choo!" This time, when he drew in a breath, it whistled alarmingly, and Mary stared at him as he staggered out of his pool. He tried to get in the sliding door that presumably led to his living room, sneezed again, struggled for breath, and slid down the slippery glass, gasping, wheezing, his face almost gray.

"Omigod, what have I done?" Mary stared at the man's form, almost feeling his awful struggle for breath, then wheeled and dashed for the door. The elevator took forever to come. Finally, the elevator doors hissed open. She lunged inside, pushed the button for the first floor, and then the one to close the doors. This was taking too long! She should have used the stairs! Surely she could have run down three flights faster than this! The sense of urgency grew and grew in her as the elevator finally came to a stop, hesitated, hitched itself up an inch or two, then reluctantly let its doors open. Before there was really enough room, she was crowding out the slender gap and flinging herself at the superintendent's door. She pounded on it with one fist, shouting his name, leaning on the bell with her free hand, praying to be heard over the high volume of his television.

"All right, all right, hold your horses." She heard Mr. Taylor shout back at her as he lumbered to the door. He opened his several locks and eased the door back an inch. From within, she heard the sound of a wildly enthusiastic voice screaming at someone to "Come on down!" As if the invitation had been meant for her, Mary shouldered the door open and went on in.

"The new tenant," she said between gasps. "He's ill. He needs help. Get a passkey and come on. Please, Mr. Taylor! We have to get him to a doctor, fast."

"What? What's that?"

"The new tenant on the second floor!" she shouted. "Give me a key to his place!"

"Oh! You've seen the stud, have you?" He laughed. "Now, Miss DeLaney, I can't give you a key to his place. Oh, you girls," he added with another laugh, slapping his fat thigh, his small eyes nearly lost in his roly-poly face. "Anything to meet the great Stud Hagendorn." He peered at her. "But I didn't think you were like that, Miss DeLaney."

"I'm not trying to meet the man, for heaven's sake! I'm trying to save his life! I tell you, he's ill!"

"Eleanor Smitherton, come on down!" the television announcer screamed, and Mr. Taylor spun to face the set, his jaw dropping.

"That's my cousin!" he said, lumbering back and slumping in his well-used chair, leaning forward, his arms on his thighs. "Look, Miss DeLaney, that's my cousin Ellie."

Of course it is, thought Mary impatiently. These were summer reruns. Mr. Taylor had seen this episode at least once before and had talked about it incessantly and with envy ever since. "Mr. Taylor! The key! Dammit, give me a key to the new tenant's suite!"

He didn't hear her, or at least didn't respond, and

Mary ran to the board on the wall where all the keys hung on little pegs. What was the name he'd said? Higgenbottom? Heatherington? Ah, here, Hagendorn. 215. Snatching up the key, she hitched her robe up and ran to the end of the hall and up the stairs at full tilt. She slid the key into the lock of 215, slapped the door open, and ran across the living room to the balcony door, where the man was still slumped, still struggling for breath.

Dragging him in with strength she hadn't known she possessed, she snatched a pillow off the sofa and thrust it under his head, tugged the headphones from around his neck and flung them aside, put another cushion under one shoulder to tilt him slightly to his side, and caught his face between her hands, shaking him to get his attention.

"Where is your puffer?" she demanded in a slow, clear voice. "You must have medication! Where is it?"

He tried to tell her, but couldn't form the words. He rolled his eyes to the left and held them there. She looked up. His bathroom. Of course. And there it was in the medicine cabinet. She flew back to his side. Poking the nozzle into his mouth, she gave him a squirt, and then another for good measure. In seconds his breathing eased, the frantic look left his eyes, the pinched tightness faded from his face, and he lay back on the pillows, clearly exhausted. His eyes closed, his long, thick, curled lashes making black arcs on his skin.

Moments later, he opened his eyes and smiled up at her. "Hey, don't look so worried, doll. I'm okay." His voice was thin, reedy.

"Sure you are," she said softly, not believing him for a minute. One of her friends had asthma, and she knew just how drained he must be feeling right now, how exhausted from fighting for breath. "Can you get up? I think you should be in bed. I'll call your doctor."

"Haven't got one," he murmured, closing his eyes again. "I'm all right, really. Just need to rest a bit."

Mary looked at the prescription label on the bronchodilator bottle she held. He had a doctor, all right. In Winnipeg. Big help. She set the bottle back on the floor beside him, touched his hand, then shook his arm. "Bruce," she said. "Come on. Let's get you to bed."

He mumbled something unintelligible, rolled a bit more to his side, drew his knees up toward his chest, and tucked one hand under his cheek. She stared at him. He looked, in that moment, very much like her friend Aggie's little boy Mark, except Mark didn't have a body like Bruce Hagendorn's, nor a desperado mustache. With a sigh, she went and got the quilt off his rumpled bed and spread it over him. Then she checked out his bathroom, finding four washcloths neatly folded on one shelf of the linen closet beside two enormous towels, and two more smaller ones. There was only one toothbrush, she noticed, as she wet a washcloth under the tap, finding some odd satisfaction in knowing he didn't share his apartment with anyone else. *Because I don't want two noisy neighbors*, she told herself—and almost believed it.

Back in the living room, she crouched down and wiped his face to remove any traces of pollen that might remain, dried his bristly skin with the towel she'd brought, then sat back on the floor. Idly picking up his headphones, she put them on and listened, a smile growing on her face.

Water lapping against a hull. The distant call of seagulls. The creak of ship's timbers. A faint wind-whistle in rigging. She laughed softly. The man was a romantic. She'd bet her last cent that he'd been sitting in that wading pool singing a gondolier's song, fantasizing himself in Venice, or on a ship far at sea, anywhere but where he'd been—in a wading pool on a westend Vancouver apartment balcony.

Picking up the portable tape player, still wearing the headphones as the mood-building sounds went on and on, Mary returned the towel and washcloth to the bathroom, hanging them neatly on the rail at the end of the vanity, then glanced around the apartment, wondering at its starkness. There was nothing that might be a clue to the personality of the man who lived there. The kitchen contained a small table and two chairs, a coffee maker on the counter, and a small microwave oven. The bedroom held only one high dresser and a huge bed and a heap of what was likely dirty laundry in one corner. The living room, containing a brown couch and two gray chairs which looked terrible on the fawn-colored carpet, was no better. There was a coffee table in front of the couch, and a smaller table near the door, and that was it. Motel modern was the only way to classify it, except it lacked even the bad oil painting screwed to the walls of most motel rooms, and the obligatory television set.

Of course, to be fair, she reminded herself that he'd only moved in last week. She gritted her teeth and glared at his recumbent form. This was two days sleep he was costing her, damn his hide! He and his deliverymen had made so much racket moving him in last Thursday, she'd only got a couple of hours sleep that day too.

Not only was the man inconsiderate, he had no taste in furniture and no sense of drama in his accessories, she thought grumpily. In fact, besides the two cushions now on the floor under him, there wasn't an accessory to be had, unless one counted the newspaper spread messily on the oblong coffee table, top section opened to the want ads, some circled in black. She bent closer, read one, then another, then blinked in disbelief and glanced over at the sleeping man under the quilt. She stared at the circled ads again.

Escort services? He was thinking of applying to an

escort service for companionship? Nope. Not that, she thought quickly, looking over at where he slept. His craggy face had a lot of charm, in spite of the fact that he had a badly bent nose. And then there was that utterly gorgeous body. The man could find companionship wherever he wanted it. He wouldn't have to rent it.

So, had he been checking out escort services for work? The thought was startling, but she had to admit it was possible. He'd obviously just moved here. It wouldn't be so strange if he were unemployed. But surely there was something else he could do?

She sighed and sat on the couch. With a name like Stud, he'd probably do very well in the escort business. Watching him sleep, she listened to the tape rewind itself and then start up again. Really, she thought, she should let herself out of this apartment, go back up to her own place, and get to bed. She'd never make it through the afternoon at the university, to say nothing of work later that night, if she didn't get some sleep. But . . . what if he needed help again? Anyway, maybe he wouldn't sleep long. Just a few minutes to regain his strength. After all, he certainly didn't look like a sickly person. He probably only had these attacks at rare intervals. Such as when someone bombarded him with pollen-laden daisies.

She sighed, feeling bad about what she'd done, but how could she have known? Still guilt clung to her, made her clench her teeth until her head ached. What if he'd died through her careless action? She shuddered, leaned over to check that he was really still breathing, and touched his cheek when he moved slightly. She jerked back, surprisingly unnerved. *Oh, cut it out,* she told herself. *You're just overtired!*

Maybe if she just lay down for a few minutes it would help. She could rest without falling asleep, couldn't she? Sure she could. For just a little while.

Then she'd wake the man up, assure herself that he wasn't going to have a relapse, and go home to bed. With a sigh, she lay down on the couch, immersed in the surf sounds and gull cries, and never even saw oblivion coming.

Stud woke slowly, disoriented, feeling a hard floor only thinly cushioned by carpet under his hip and shoulder. He was covered by a thick blanket of some sort. Hot! Damn, but it was hot in there. The sun was beating in through the patio doors, flooding the room with heat and light. He shoved the quilt back. And what was he doing on the floor? Was it even his floor? Cushions. He patted one of them. Yes. His cushions. Cream and brown alternate squares. He remembered buying them on impulse a few days ago when he'd seen a big bin of them in a drugstore. Maybe they'd make his new apartment look a little bit less institutional, he'd thought then. They really hadn't helped a whole lot. Maybe he'd spent so much of his life living in hotel rooms, every place he was going to live for the rest of his life was going to look like one. He felt a wave of loneliness and homesickness wash over him and fought it down. After all, he was a grown man, thirty-six years old. He could live without his family around. He'd done it for years. But then, he reminded himself, he'd had a home to go to between times.

His eyes lit on his inhaler sitting beside him on the floor, and he frowned. What was that doing out? He didn't remember needing it, but obviously he had. Could a guy overdose on Ventolin? Nah! He shook his head, rubbed his eyes, started to sit up, and then stopped. His eyes widened as he took in the sight of a small, shapely foot with neatly trimmed toenails gleaming bright pink only a few inches from his face. Above that, as his disbelieving eyes tracked upward, was a long, slender, bare, and distinctly feminine leg draped down off the edge of his couch. The knee of that leg was as smooth as the curving calf, and the thigh disappeared into a froth of scarlet lace edging the hem of a short black nightgown.

Well! Slowly Stud got to his feet, swayed a bit, then steadied as he looked down at the beautiful woman on his couch. Her other leg, stretched along the cushions of the sofa, was as pretty as the one he'd first seen. He wanted, suddenly, to touch them both, to run his hands up those smooth, creamy thighs, right to where that black lace teased him with visions of what might lie beyond, and . . .

The prim, high-necked blue chenille robe she wore was at complete odds with what he could see of that sexy little nightgown its parted front revealed. He deliberately moved his gaze from those long, long legs, concentrating on her face, hoping that might help him remember. Her full lips were slightly open, lush and pink and extremely kissable. Her dark lashes were long and thick and tipped with gold. Her brown hair, while not as dark as his, was long and curled in a tumble over one shoulder. Her face was slender, with high, slanted cheekbones and a pointed chin. A beauty, for sure. But where had he found her, and why had she been sleeping on the couch and he on the floor, when there was a perfectly good bed only a few feet away?

She woke, not as he had, dull-witted and disoriented, but completely, all at once. He watched her eyes widen as realization dawned that she was sprawled, legs apart, robe open almost from the waist down, before a strange man who stood gazing at her in appreciation. With a gasp, she sat up in one fluid motion as she pulled her robe closed over legs she pressed firmly together, crossed at the ankles as she stared up at him and pushed his headphones off her ears.

"Oh," she said. "Are you all right? Feeling better?"

He smiled, his head cocked to one side. "I feel

great. In fact, I'm feeling better by the minute. But I'd sure like to know who you are, doll, and what you're doing here."

"What?" She got to her feet, coming up much shorter than he'd anticipated, considering those long legs of hers. "Don't you remember?"

"I remember waking up all cocooned in a quilt, sweating like a pig, and seeing your very pretty leg hanging off the couch. You're welcome to sleep on my couch anytime, but I'd kind of like to know your name."

"Mary DeLaney. I'm a neighbor. I helped you. You were . . . sick."

He glanced down at his inhaler. "Oh. Yeah. But what . . ." Damn, how corny could a guy get? He'd almost said, "What happened?"

As if he had, she said, "I threw some daisies at you, and you had an asthma attack."

His eyes narrowed as he thought, then opened wider when he remembered. "Oh, yeah!" His eyes were, she now noticed, a shade of hazel-green that went well with his slightly olive skin and dark hair. "What in hell did you do that for? Flinging flowers in a guy's face isn't one of the recommended ways of getting introduced. Not," he added, "when the water they were in is still attached."

"I wasn't angling for an introduction," she said, tilting her chin up as she glared at him. Something Mr. Taylor had said came back to her. Something about "all the girls wanting to meet the stud," or words to that effect. She blinked as she looked at this man. He was tall—nearly a foot taller than she was—and his tight, brightly patterned swimsuit didn't hide a thing. She took in his slender hips, muscular thighs, well-defined chest, and shoulders that begged to have hands curl around them. His forearms and legs were liberally covered with curly hair and his head with thick, dark hair, no curl. Long, thick lashes shadowed eyes that held a sparkle of good humor. Did he look familiar? Should she know who he was?

He grinned cockily. He knew she was cataloguing his looks and simply accepted it as his due. He'd been looked at before and learned to like it. And that name—Stud Hagendorn. She frowned. Was it one she should recognize? Something told her yes, but she still couldn't place it. Stud! Lord, what a thing to call someone. How he must hate it.

"Well?" he said, as he struck a bodybuilder's pose. "What do you think?" On second thought, maybe he didn't hate it.

He watched her chin tilt up another quarter inch, watched color rise in her face and chagrin flood those pretty blue eyes, but she met his gaze as she retorted, "I think you have a severe allergy to flowers, and that you should have a doctor a lot closer than Winnipeg."

Okay, he thought, *she's embarrassed that I picked up on her staring but not intimidated in the least.* That was good. He didn't want to intimidate her. He wanted to kiss her, hold her slender body in his arms, touch her skin because it looked silky smooth and rich and alive and warmly welcoming. She was beautiful, this Mary DeLaney, in her prim-and-proper bathrobe with that damn sexy nightgown hidden away. He grinned again. No way was he going to forget it was there. He looked at her as if she weren't wearing the robe over it, and saw her flush again. *A shy one!*

"Now you're staring," she said briskly. "Why don't you have a doctor here?"

"There hasn't been time, and I haven't needed one. But you're right; I should have one, and I mean to see to it soon. Who do you recommend? How about yours?"

She had to laugh. "I don't think my gynecologist would have a lot of interest in your lungs." *But she'd probably admire your chest*, she added silently.

A shy one with a sense of humor! He liked her laugh, husky, throaty, and sexy as hell. It reminded him again of that nightgown she was hiding, and he hadn't needed any reminders. "So. I guess I'll rely on the yellow pages. Why *did* you empty your vase on me?"

"You were singing. At least that's what you called it," she told him. "I had to get your attention somehow. I needed to sleep. I'd been up all night at work, and I have a class at three—" Her eyes widened even more. "Oh, Lord! What time is it?" she asked, realizing that the sun was now coming directly in the patio doors as it only did in midafternoon.

Frantically, she looked at her wrist where her watch should have been, only it was on her bedside table, the alarm set for two o'clock so she could make her three-thirty class.

"Does it matter?" he asked, sitting down on the arm of the sofa, crossing his arms over his chest, liking the way color ebbed and flowed over her high cheekbones, the way shadows moved within the depths of her blue eyes. "What's your hurry, Mary DeLaney? Sit down. Stay and get acquainted now that you're here. I'd offer you a cup of coffee, but I don't have any yet. I've just moved out here from Win—"

She snatched his wrist in both hands, turning it over so she could see the face of his watch, and then she gasped, spinning away from him. "Oh, darn it! I'm going to be late!"

Spotting the key she'd swiped from the superintendent, she picked it up from the little table where it lay and tossed it to him. "Return that to Mr. Taylor, okay?" she said, and then she was gone.

Stud stared at the door she had slammed behind her, feeling bereft and wondering what in the hell had just hit him. His wrist tingled where her hands had encircled it. His heart was hammering. His chest felt tight, but not as if he needed a blast from his puffer. He slumped down on the couch where she'd been sleeping, and shook his head. Then, stretching out, he smelled the perfume she'd left behind. For a moment, he simply lay there and breathed it in, then got resolutely to his feet. Taylor would be able to tell him all about her.

Mary groaned as she twisted the doorknob of her apartment and bashed her shoulder against it, all to no avail. She'd locked herself out. Muttering dark things about asthmatic men who caused more trouble than they were worth, she marched back to the elevator, which by some miracle was still on her floor, and got in, punching the button for the main floor. It stopped on the second, and hissed open to admit the man she had just been reviling.

"I like this building more and more," he said conversationally. "You, Mary DeLaney, are a bonus I didn't expect. Do you always wear your nightclothes while traveling up and down in the elevator?" He leered as he said "nightclothes," and she remembered the look she'd seen on his face when she'd woken up on his couch. She remembered, too, her state of dishabille.

"Of course not," she said crossly. "I'm locked out. When I went to help you, I never even thought about my own key." The elevator opened, and she stepped out briskly, overly conscious of her bare feet, her long blue robe, and even more aware of his eyes on her. He knew that under the decent covering was that indecent scrap of red and black that she'd been unable to resist when it had gone on sale at Woodwards.

"No, Cruz! You can't mean that!" cried a passionate female voice through the door of the super's apartment. There was a sob and another sound she couldn't identify, but Mary ignored the pathos and hammered with her fist, the other hand taking care of the doorbell, hoping to quickly drag Mr. Taylor from his soaps.

"I'm coming, I'm coming," he shouted finally, and she felt as much as heard his footsteps as he thudded toward the door. "Whaddya—Oh. Miss DeLaney. What is it this time? Wouldn't the stud let you in? That's prob'ly just as well, I gotta say. You're not the type to—"

"Mr. Taylor, I'm locked out. May I have a key, please? I'm going to be late for class and—" But Mr. Taylor wasn't even listening. His small eyes brightened as he looked over Mary's shoulder.

"Hey! Stud! Howya doin', boy? Whaddaya think? You don't mind that she took your key, do you? I mean, you're going to meet all the women in the building anyway, so why not start out right away? Once they know you're here, you'll be gettin' invites for dinner, knocks on your door wantin' to borrow cups of coffee and sugar, and—"

"Mr. Taylor, I need a key!" Mary shouted, but he was still beaming over her shoulder at the tall man who stood, Mary ascertained with a quick glance, grinning like a lunatic.

"Ohhh!" she said, shoving past Mr. Taylor and lifting the key to her own apartment from the board while he went on gabbing to the man he persisted in calling "Stud."

Didn't Bruce Hagendorn see that as an insult? She certainly thought it was one, but it wasn't her worry, she decided, neatly slipping past both men again and dashing for the elevator.

It took her all of three minutes to shower, and only another four to dress, because she neglected to bundle her long hair up in the back as she normally did. She flew out the door, running down the stairs instead of waiting for the elevator, and across the wide parking area in front of the building. She jogged to the bus stop, praying that the bus she usually took had been held up somewhere, so she wouldn't have a fifteen-minute wait for the next one. With a groan, she rounded the corner and saw the bus's rear end swaying away from her, half a block ahead. Even knowing it was futile, she still ran, clutching her books to her chest, hoping against hope that the driver would see her in his mirror and wait at the corner. He didn't.

Leaning back against a light pole, she sighed, blowing her bangs off her forehead, lifting the heavy mane of hair from her neck with her free hand. Damn, it was too hot to be running after buses. Besides, she hadn't had enough sleep, her head ached, and she wasn't going to be able to concentrate at all today. "And it's all Bruce Hagendorn's fault."

Two

"Come on, doll," said that very man from right beside her. "I'll drive you to wherever it is you have to go, since you seem to think it's my fault you're late."

She lifted her head. At least he had clothes on. Jeans. A green shirt that made his eyes more green than hazel. A denim jacket. He smiled, and his black mustache twitched. At the curb stood a huge black motorcycle, its engine running surprisingly quietly, but with a deep throb that suggested far too much power.

He bowed, gestured toward the machine, and said, "M'lady?"

She gaped. "Are you kidding? On that?"

His smile faded. He looked hurt. "It's the best I can do."

"But I don't know how to ride one of those."

"That's okay," he said gently. "I do. I know how to do lots of things."

I'll just bet you do, she thought, and wondered why that made her feel sad and angry all at the same time. And oddly threatened.

"Come on," he urged her. "It'll be fun."

"No," she said. And then added, just a trifle ungraciously, "Thanks. It doesn't look like fun to me."

17

"Okay. If you'd rather be late." He shrugged but didn't leave.

She frowned, thinking about Professor Harder, who was well named. Dr. Katherine Harder, her advisor, did not like to be kept waiting. Mary bit her lip, glanced uneasily from man to machine. They seemed to go together too well, both large, both rumbling with quiet, leashed power, both ultimately dangerous. If that was her best way of getting to her appointment on time, maybe it would simply be easier to forget her doctoral studies, ignore the thesis yet to be written, pretend Professor Harder had never been born. But . . .

She sighed. Getting through this last year at the university was something she wanted very, very badly. She was so far behind her contemporaries. Not that she saw the time she'd spent out of school as wasted, but she was desperate to catch up. She'd come this far. Wasn't it worth one more small sacrifice?

She looked at her wrist. Her watch was still in her bedroom, but she knew she was going to be disastrously late if she waited for the next bus. She looked at the bike. She looked at the man. She swallowed hard, then made up her mind. "All right, then," she said in a rush before she could wimp out. She hated being a coward and knew that too often in the past four years she had let her irrational fears rule her. "Thank you. What do I have to do?"

He smiled, his eyes going warmer and darker, and she felt rewarded somehow, as if he'd recognized the courage it had taken her to reach a decision and acknowledged it. "You put this on," he said, unstrapping a red helmet from behind the seat. Carefully, he slipped it over her hair and tucked the strands back out of his way so he could fasten the strap under her chin. A little shudder ran irrepressibly through her at his touch. "And this." He gave her his denim jacket.

"No! That's yours," she said, trying to fight off his attempt to put it on her.

"You have short sleeves," he said, touching her arm below the edge of her yellow blouse, his hand lingering as if he liked the feel of her skin. Her heart literally stopped beating for a moment. "You need it more than I do." He pulled it around her and shoved her arms into the sleeves.

The sleeves of his green shirt were rolled up above his elbows, and he proceeded to roll them down and button the cuffs. "I hate being hit by stinging bugs," he said. "Now you sit up here." He lifted her unexpectedly as if she weren't five feet four and a hundred and eighteen pounds, and sat her astride the wide black seat. Tugging on his own helmet, he sat in front of her.

"You can hang on here, behind you," he said, half-turning and touching the small arched support at her back, "or you can put your arms around my waist."

Tilting her chin up, she clasped her hands firmly on the rear backrest. He grinned knowingly, as if he'd had no doubt which option she'd choose, then turned to the front again and revved the motor. He eased the bike forward, found a slot in traffic, and headed west on West Fourth, in the direction of the university. Sitting stiffly, she tried to keep the insides of her knees from touching his hips, tried to keep her body out of contact in all ways, but it was difficult. Only by staying absolutely rigid could she maintain an aloof posture.

Then, so suddenly she had to muffle a scream of terror, he gunned the engine, swayed the bike, and shot out around a slow-moving bus.

My bus! Mary thought in amazement, seeing the number on its rear end flash by. But then Bruce twisted their path once more, and she fought the sway of the bike, feeling as if she were about to fall, then flung her arms around his middle, clinging like a limpet as he jumped ahead to make a light that was about to change.

"Sway with me!" he shouted into the slipstream, taking one hand off the controls of the bike long enough to pat her hands as they linked across his belly. "Don't try to fight the motion!"

It was easier, she found, when she did as he said. As they accelerated through traffic, then slowed for corners and curved smoothly around them, she moved with him, feeling the warm security of his back against her front, and feeling a whole lot more that she hadn't felt in some time, that she hadn't wanted to feel, because feeling was something she tried to keep to a minimum these days. It scared her and thrilled her and excited her, and she wanted it never to end even while she was praying that they'd get there fast so she could get away from him before she disgraced herself entirely by sliding her hands up his chest to feel him through the thin fabric of his shirt.

When he stopped for a light just before the entrance to the university, he turned and said, "What building are we aiming for? I'm not familiar with this territory yet." But he was, she decided, familiar with having a woman behind him on his bike. The glitter in his eyes told her he was enjoying having her hold onto him a lot more than she was enjoying having to do it. Or a lot more than she told herself she was enjoying it.

She gave him concise instructions, and then they were off again. When he halted once more and lifted his helmet off, Mary was surprised to discover they had arrived already.

Removing her own helmet and getting shakily from the bike, she managed a smile. "Thank you. That was . . ." She bit her lip, not sure how to describe the experience.

"Fun?" he suggested gently.

"Oh! No," she said, faintly offended that he should think she'd have found riding a motorcycle with him, clinging to him, "fun."

"It was different. Something I'd never done before, but . . ."

"But what?"

Yes, Mary, she asked herself. *But what?* But . . . No, there could be no buts in her thoughts. *To thine own self be true.* How many times had her grandmother said that to her? Okay, she'd found the bike ride stimulating, exciting, thrilling if a little bit scary. And, she was forced to admit, even if only to herself, it had been fun. As she made the admission to herself, she had to acknowledge her surprise. Was she so repressed, so full of fears, that she didn't want to take any enjoyment from life anymore? She bit her lip and looked at the man who stood waiting patiently for her to say something. She tried to, opened her mouth, but no words came out, so she closed it again.

When he lifted one brow and gave her a quizzical look, she knew she owed him the truth. She sighed and gave in. "I . . . yes, all right, it was fun." She laughed a trifle self-consciously, then felt a huge and genuine smile cover her face. "A lot of fun!" She shrugged out of the overlarge denim jacket and held it out toward him.

He took it and draped it over the seat of the bike. "Good," he said, and touched her chin with the tips of two fingers. "I'm glad it was fun for you, because it sure was fun for me." Something inside her quivered with pleasure, and the muscles of her legs remembered too well the feel of his hard body between them. Her breath caught in her throat. She moved back from him. He wasn't deterred in the least; he followed, tracing a light pattern over her shoulder. "And we'll do it again," he said. "What time will you be finished here?"

She hesitated for only a moment. "Six, but then I have to go to work."

"Where do you work?"

"Uh . . . downtown." She preferred not to tell people where she worked. It raised too many eyebrows.

"I'll be back here at six," he said, then touched her again, this time drawing those same two fingers from her temple to the collar of her yellow blouse.

Again, she stepped back, flinching slightly at the stab of sensation that zipped through her body.

He looked troubled. "Don't you like to be touched?"

She blinked at him. "I . . . don't know. I've never given it much thought." Of course she had. She'd liked the way Kevin touched her, missed that desperately along with him, but that was in the past. Since then she hadn't let anyone get close enough to touch. She hadn't wanted to. So why was this man right inside her personal space? She hardly knew him. She certainly shouldn't be responding to him like this. Normally she had to know a man for a long time, and know him well, before she felt anything for him. Yet with Bruce Hagendorn . . .

"You feel so nice, I like to touch you," he said. "But if it makes you uncomfortable, I'll try to remember not to do it until you're more relaxed with me. And I'll be back here, in this very spot, at six."

"Bruce . . ."

"Yuk! Don't call me that!" he said, his nose wrinkling in distaste.

"Why? It's your name, isn't it? That's what it said on the label of your Ventolin."

"It's the name my mother gave me. A sissy name. I hate it."

"What's sissy about it?"

"I don't know. It just is. All the Bruces I ever met were wimpy. Except me, of course," he added with a grin she was compelled to return.

"Didn't you ever hear of Robert the Bruce?"

His eyes danced as he replied, "No. Should I have?"

"Maybe not, unless you've studied Scottish history. He was a great Scots hero, a king. He won the battle of Bannockburn and freed Scotland from the English."

"Great," said Stud. "The hero I'm named for wore a skirt? I'm supposed to find some comfort in that?"

She laughed, as he'd hoped she would. He liked the sound of her laughter. "I don't answer to that name," he said. "My friends call me Stud."

"*I* won't!" she blurted out before she could stop herself.

"Why not?" He wrapped one of her curls around his finger, smoothing the hair over his knuckle with his thumb, as his hand brushed her throat like a soft kiss. "Aren't you going to be my friend?"

She opened her mouth to tell him why not, but couldn't. With two fingers of his free hand, he shut her mouth for her, lifting her chin and holding it.

Once more she moved away, but not, Stud noticed with satisfaction, quite as quickly as before, and he didn't think that was all to do with his having a grip on her hair. Slowly, he let his hands drop. Her mouth stayed shut. The ringlet he had made bobbed in front of her ear, and she tucked it impatiently behind. "It's a terrible nickname, is why not! Why do you put up with it? I mean, it's demeaning. It's as bad as if you were to call me 'hot-pants' or something along those lines. Aren't you more than just . . . that?"

He grinned. "Probably. Are you interested in finding out?"

The bus she should have been on trundled around the corner and came to a halt, breathing its diesel breath like a dragon poisoning its enemies. She was happy to see it.

"I have to go now," she said, then remembered. "Oh, would you be kind enough to return this to Mr. Taylor? He gets really upset if he doesn't get the extra key back right away." She dug it out of her pocket and handed it to him. "Good-bye, Bruce. And thanks for the lift."

"Stud," he corrected her. "See you at six."

She had the distinct impression he just barely bit back his temptation to say, "*See you at six . . . hot-pants.*"

"*Who is Stud Hagendorn?*" Keith stared at Mary from behind his thick glasses. "I can't believe you said that! Where have you spent your life, for pete's sake? Living in a cave? Mary, Mary, so damn contrary. When do you plan to move into the real world? There's more to life than work and study, you know."

He'd given up seriously trying to date her long ago, but once in a while he hinted that with some encouragement he'd ask again.

She did know that most people had fuller lives than she did, at least more varied lives. She just didn't have the time or energy for anything but the two activities that occupied her days and nights. Still, that didn't mean she couldn't take a casual interest in her new neighbor, did it?

"So who is he?"

Keith sighed. "He's just one of the best known hockey players in the country, is all! Or he was until he retired a couple of years ago, long before anyone expected him to. He lives somewhere on the prairies. Why?"

"He doesn't. He lives here. In my building. I met him, that's all. And I got the impression I should have known who he was, and I didn't, so I asked you. I wanted an answer, not a lecture on my lifestyle. I don't watch hockey."

"Or read newspapers, or follow the news on TV or radio, or simply listen to your fellowman talk, obviously," said her friend scathingly, shaking his head. "Hey, Mary. Invite me over one day, will you? I'd like to meet him."

"Maybe. How did he get the nickname Stud?"

Keith grinned. "You have to ask?"

Pulling a face, she said, "I guess not." She remembered the want ads he'd circled, and sighed silently, wishing for some reason that it were otherwise, but at that moment the professor's door opened and another doctoral candidate came out. Mary waited a moment, then stood and knocked before entering, emptying her mind of everything but the project she was to discuss with Dr. Harder.

She allowed it to drift, though, as she walked out of the building several hours later after the seminar she'd led, only half-listening to the conversation of her students making plans for the evening. It was Friday evening, and everyone had dates. Everyone but her. It had never mattered before, and she wouldn't let it matter now. There was no reason why it should, was there? Besides, she did have a date. A date with her job.

Keith was right though. She might as well have been living in a cave these past four years. Here she was, twenty-nine years old, a graduate student who did nothing but work and study and sleep. It wasn't much of a life, but it was the only one she could foresee for the next six months or so. But, she had to admit, she was tired. So damned tired. It would be nice to relax, to play, to drift now and then.

She sank down onto a gritty bench in the bus shelter and let her eyes wander along the tree-lined avenue, waiting for the bus to come. Her watch was still on her bedside table, but it couldn't be much after six. She'd have time for a quick bite in the coffee shop next door to the center or maybe even one of Mr. Leung's special noodle dishes filled with fresh prawns. Friday nights were often heavy, and she wasn't looking forward to this one; she was going into it too tired. Last night had been hell, and Wednesday, the day welfare checks were distributed, double hell. And thanks to Caruso, she'd lost quite a bit of sleep. She didn't think the few hours she'd caught on his couch really counted. She'd need to stoke her furnace if she were to weather another night like the previous two. Where was that bus?

It was a motorcycle that came to a halt beside her, and a grinning Bruce Hagendorn who swung his long leg over the seat, bowing before her as he had before. "M'lady?" he said again. At that moment, the bus made its wheezy way around the corner and toward the stop.

"Hurry up," said Stud, glancing over his shoulder at it. "Let's go before I get ticketed."

"But that's my bus. . . ."

He picked her up as he'd done before, set her astride the seat, and hopped on, roaring out of the bus zone just in time. Then, pulling over again, he jumped off, put a jacket on her—a spare one he'd had tied around his waist by its sleeves—plopped the red helmet over her hair, and fastened the chin strap.

"Why?" Mary asked of no one in particular. "Why am I letting the man do this?"

"Because he's sexy and irresistible," Bruce said with a grin as he took her books and stuffed them into the compartment at the back. "And soon to be a partner in his very own business. Sexy, irresistible, independent businessmen are—well, let's face it, Mary DeLaney—irresistible." He remounted the bike and fired it up once more. "Hang on," he ordered, and she did, mulling over his words. Sexy and irresistible? He had an inflated opinion of himself, didn't he? But, dammit, he was absolutely right. He was certainly sexy, and she wasn't having much luck resisting him, was she?

"And," he shouted over his shoulder as they pulled away from the curb, "because you and I are destined to be friends, sweet Mary. And friends help each other out."

Friends? she thought, leaning lightly against his back, head ducked down out of the wind. It was a long time since she'd had anything but the most casual of friendships with anyone but Aggie, with whom she'd been pals since second grade. Her life-style didn't lend itself to an active social life.

"What time do you have to be at work?" he asked moments later, turning as they waited for a light.

"Seven-thirty, but—"

"Do you have to go home first?"

"No, but—"

"Good. Then there's plenty of time for dinner. Where do you want to go? Some place quick and casual, please. I'm not dressed for nice."

"Bruce . . ."

"Hey, come on, doll. I'm a stranger in town. I'm lonely. Please?"

How could she refuse such a plea? Besides, the light at right angles was amber, and theirs was about to turn green. "There's a White Spot about six blocks straight ahead."

"Right. White Spot, here we come."

He pushed his empty plate away and cradled his coffee cup in two hands, his greenish eyes glittering as he looked at her. "That," he said, "is the best damn hamburger I've ever eaten, and likely the mess-iest. Do they do breakfasts too?"

Mary shrugged. She had no idea, but a passing waitress smiled at him and said, "Great breakfasts, sir." She looked at him more closely. "You know, you look an awful lot like that hockey player. Stud something."

He nodded. "Lots of people tell me that. But I think my mustache is a little shorter and neater."

"Yeah . . . I think so too. Still . . . it's a strong resemblance. Maybe you're related?"

He shrugged. "Could be. I do have family in Manitoba. That's where he's from, isn't it?"

The woman shook her head. "I don't really know. I don't watch hockey. I've just seen his picture now and then, and watched if he was being interviewed on the news. Anyway, even if you're not him, you're welcome here for breakfast. You'll find something good on the menu. I guarantee it personally."

"Can't ask for more than that," he responded, returning her smile. "We'll be here."

"You might be, but I won't," said Mary quickly. She thought that given the least bit of encouragement the waitress might just put herself on the menu for Bruce Hagendorn's breakfast. She also thought there was something vaguely sinful in having breakfast in a restaurant unless one were traveling. She frowned at him.

"Why did you lie to her?"

He lifted his brows. "Did I?"

She thought back and then shook her head. "No. Not exactly. Except about the length of the mustache."

He grinned, and that mustache twitched, bracketing the corners of his mouth. "It was bushier a few years back. I keep it trimmed now. Makes me look more . . . respectable."

"It does?" Mary blurted out.

He laughed. "You don't think so? What do you think of it?"

"Well . . ."

"Come on, don't worry about hurting my feelings. I've got a hard shell."

She didn't really believe that for some reason, but he had asked. "It makes you look like a . . . desperado. Like you should wear a black hat."

He chuckled. "And carry guns low on my hips?"

"Something like that," she said with a rueful smile.

"Want me to shave it off?"

"What? No! Of course not."

"I'd do it, if it would make you like me better," he said, and when she failed to reply, he touched the back of her hand, drawing the caress out the full length of her index finger and over her neatly trimmed nail. "Will you have breakfast with me in the morning? If not here, then someplace else?"

She remembered his having said earlier that he didn't even have coffee in his apartment. Did he eat all his meals out? "Don't you cook?"

"Not unless I have to," he said. "I can do it, but I hate cleaning up afterward. What time do you finish work?"

"Seven-thirty," she said, making him frown.

"A twelve-hour shift? What is this place, anyway, a sweatshop?"

She raised her brows. "That's as good a description as any, I suppose, only I'm not the one who does most of the sweating. Wednesdays to Saturdays I'm night supervisor in a detox center."

He stared. She sighed. She was used to that reaction.

"Detoxification? Drugs?"

"Some. Mostly alcohol, though. It's the drug of preference for the people down there. It's about all that they can afford. Cheap, rotgut rum, Chinese cooking wine, homemade stuff, shoe polish, shaving lotion."

"Why do you work there?"

She shook her head. "I often ask myself that, but the answer is that I don't know. Because somebody has to, I suppose. Because somebody has to care," she added, almost fiercely.

"Well, it shouldn't be you." He eyed her narrowly, then startled her by saying, "You care too much."

She was amazed at his perception, and was thoughtful for a moment, looking up at him before she said, "I care, all right, but no one can care 'too much' about something like that. I believe that alcoholism is the scourge of our times! It is my dearest wish that by some miracle, all alcoholic beverages could be banned forever from this earth!"

"But—" But it's been tried, he was about to say, only she lifted a hand and swept on, her eyes blazing.

"Alcohol causes too many problems, ruins too many lives. It's an evil that should be eradicated. If it were just being invented now, it would never be allowed on the market—it's too dangerous—but because it's been around for so long, and because there are so many powerful corporations and greedy individuals earning profits from it, it's here to stay even though it screws up lives daily, hourly."

"Greedy individuals? People wouldn't sell booze if there weren't a market for it, you know. It's what the public wants and—"

"I know, but 'the public,' or part of it, wants heroin, too, but they can't have it legally, can they?"

He stared at her. "You equate alcohol with heroin?"

"Yes. And I equate the people who make their living poisoning others in the full knowledge that they are doing so with drug dealers. They don't care what happens to their customers as long as they get to rake in their cash. I think they should all be jailed, at the very least."

His dark brows drew together, and he looked at her from under them, not happy with her statement. "Wow! That's a hard line to take. Not everyone who takes a drink becomes an alcoholic."

She subsided. "I know that. Intellectually, I do,

but in here," she tapped her chest with her finger-
nails, "I hate it so much that I want to stamp it out
entirely." To her horror, her voice wobbled slightly,
and her eyes glazed over with tears that she blinked
back quickly. His frown faded until his look held
nothing but compassion.

His hand was warm over hers. "Why, Mary? What
happened to make you feel that way?"

She didn't want to tell him, but the words wouldn't
stop. "My father was an alcoholic. He fell asleep—no,
there's no way to pretty it up, and no need—he
passed out one Christmas Eve with a cigarette in
his hand. They said later it lit the paper on a pack-
age under the tree, then lit the tree itself. I was
seven, and I remember my mother shouting, screaming at him to wake up, and her snatching me out of
bed and throwing me out a window to someone
outside. People were screaming at her to get out,
too, but she went back for my dad. They found them
both on the floor near the back door, so close to
safety. She'd been trying to drag him out, when the
fumes and smoke overcame her. I still see those
lights, the flames, hear the noises, hear her calling
over and over to my father, but it was no use. His
alcoholism killed them both." She shuddered, felt
the strength of his grip on her hand, the warmth of
it, and was grateful.

She drew in a deep breath. "And then—" She broke
off, knowing she couldn't go on. She bit down on a
knuckle, trying to steady herself. *That* was something she was most definitely not going to talk about
over dinner with a casual acquaintance. Bad enough
she'd spouted off all the rest of it. It must be because
she was overtired, she decided, still feeling ashamed
of her spiel. Heck, she never did that! Well, except
maybe when she was arguing with someone she
knew well, like Aggie and her husband, Steve. There
had been times she and Ag and Steve had really
gotten into it.

"And then . . . what?" Bruce said softly, encouragingly, bringing her mind back to the here and now.

"And then my grandparents came and got me, and made my life very happy and secure for the next thirteen years."

Stud looked at her hard. That was not what she'd been about to say, and he knew it. There was more to this story than the lady was willing to share right now. It didn't matter. He had time. Though why he wanted to take the time, he couldn't have said. Normally, when a woman's opinions were so completely opposite to his own, he steered clear. Yet this time, something was different.

"Your grandparents raised you?"

She smiled and nodded. "They were wonderful, and I loved them so much! They loved me, too, but couldn't live without each other. Grandpa died within three months of Gran's death, when I was in my second year at the university." She bit her lip, looked down at the table, then shook her head as if to clear it. With a quick smile, she glanced up at him and drew her hand from under his. "Sorry," she said. "I seldom talk about that, and I don't usually expound on my hatred of alcohol, either. I just do what I can to alleviate some of the problems it creates, and down there, where I work, there are plenty of problems."

"You say, 'down there.' Down where?" he asked.

"Downtown, east side."

Again, he frowned at her from under his dark brows. "I may not have been here in Vancouver very long, Mary DeLaney, but even a newcomer knows that's skid row."

She smiled again. "You certainly are a newcomer if you're still saying 'skid *row*,' Easterner. The correct term is skid *road*. It goes back to when Vancouver wasn't even Vancouver but was just a little logging village. The logs were skidded from the bush to the water along what was called the skid road. Loggers and other not-so-elegant people lived alongside, drinking and carousing and whooping it up when they weren't working. The term skid road for the worst part of town originated out here on the Pacific coast. Vancouver had one, so did Seattle. You people from back east corrupted it in your woeful ignorance," she concluded with a snooty sniff, and a twitch of her small nose.

He laughed in appreciation. "Well, la-de-da! And for your information, Winnipeg is considered a part of the West, so you can hardly call me an Easterner."

"From my point of view, it's about as far east as I ever want to go. After all," she added with a grin, "it's on the wrong side of the Rockies."

"Lotusland snob."

"Yup."

He laughed softly. "I like you, Mary DeLaney."

She couldn't speak for a minute or two. Then, in a voice that cracked a little, she said, "I like you, too, Bruce Hagendorn," vaguely surprised to find that it was true. She'd really enjoyed her dinner with him, and riding his bike, talking to him, laughing over nothing and anything. It had been so very long since she'd done anything remotely like this. She considered whether or not she felt any kind of residual guilt, decided she didn't, and was glad. After four years, she shouldn't. The psychologist in her knew that; it was the widow part of her that had a few doubts.

"I'd like you a whole lot better if you wouldn't call me Bruce, though," he said, interrupting her thoughts.

"Sorry. I refuse to call a man Stud."

His grin was all male and elicited a distinctly female response in her, one that tingled and burned and made her itch far inside. She shifted in the padded booth. "Maybe someday you'll change your mind." She didn't think there was any doubt in his mind in spite of his use of the word "maybe."

"Not a chance!" She glanced at the clock on the wall of the restaurant. "And now I have to go. Thank you for dinner, Bruce. That was a rare treat."

"I'll drive you," he said. 'Since I let you distract me from objecting to where you work, the least you can do is permit me to see that you get there safely."

She shook her head. "There's no need. I can take a taxi from here. It's subsidized."

"Not tonight," he said, taking her hand in his as they stood. "Tonight, indulge me. It may be my last chance to escort you around town for a while. Tomorrow I think I'll be working, if everything goes right."

"Good for you! What will you be doing?"

He looked a trifle vague. "I'm . . . not sure it'll pan out."

"I see." She could relate to a person not wanting to discuss something prematurely. And he'd said he might be entering into a partnership. A partnership in an escort service? Maybe he was simply embarrassed to say so. She certainly would be. Still, it wasn't her business, and it was his right not to talk about it. "Well, I wish you luck, whatever it is you end up doing, but I really do have to get going."

He stood as she did. "You'll let me give you a ride?"

"Well . . ." she said, thinking about being behind him on that bike, about having her body pressed against his. "Okay. Thanks."

She wondered at the casual ease with which he retained her hand in his as he paid the bill and walked outside. She wondered about him, period. He seemed to be an expert at parrying questions about himself. She supposed that came from being a sports celebrity. Mostly they'd talked about her and her studies, the classes she taught, and her work at the center, which surprised her. Normally she didn't like to talk about herself, but with him it seemed easy. He thought psychology was a fascinating subject. He'd had dealings with a sports psychologist, he said, but mostly he just wanted to listen to her. It was as if he found *her* fascinating, too, and it was a long time since anyone had. She got on the bike behind him, wrapped her arms around him, and dreamed a few tiny, illicit dreams, though why she should consider them illicit, she couldn't have said. It was just that she was out of the habit of dreaming, and anyway, the man had only offered her friendship. Hadn't he?

Three

"I really hate leaving you here," Stud said, pulling up in front of the center, glancing around at the seedy neighborhood. The center, though, had clean windows, a sturdy door, and bright lights over the sidewalk, to say nothing of the prominent sign stating that there were no drugs at all kept on the premises. He took some comfort in that.

"I've been coming here four nights a week for the past four years," Mary said, taking off her helmet and handing it to him. Why was he acting like this? They had met only that morning, yet he seemed to want her to think he truly cared about her and her safety. She wasn't used to it and found it touched something soft deep inside her, something she tried to harden as she peeled off his jacket as well, offering it back to him.

He wouldn't take it. "You'll need that in the morning when I come for you."

"You don't have to come for me! What if this job pans out? Won't you be going to work?"

"Not until later. I'll be working nights, too, Mary, if I take it." He smiled and touched her cheek with those two fingers of his that he seemed unable to control. "Gives us lots of time to get to know each other, play a little, have some fun together." He paused. "Eat breakfast together."

"I don't eat breakfast, and I sleep during the day." Odd that he should use that word "play." She had used it herself only a few hours before in thinking about her sterile, lonely life. And him.

"You have to wake up sometime," he said.

"When I do, I go out to class. And then to work. If I'm not doing one or the other of those, I'm studying at home. I don't have time to play." Even to her, her voice sounded faintly desperate, as if she were trying to convince herself as well as him.

"You can study all night," he countered, flicking her earlobe before dropping his hand. "You already told me you did that, so you can't go back on it now."

"Friday and Saturday nights I rarely have time to study," she said, trying to counter the breathless feeling inside her chest by drawing in a deep gulp of air. It didn't help. She drew in another as his fingers curled around her neck briefly. Dammit, he was the touchingest man! And she was going to hyperventilate at any moment, if she didn't watch herself. She pulled herself free, stepping away.

"Thanks again, Bruce. Good night."

"Stud," he said, his eyes on her lips as if he were considering kissing her.

She quickly shook her head and gave him a nervous smile, then turned and went inside the center.

Mary barely glanced at Joe, her colleague, who looked up from the desk as she walked by. She stood in the staff room for several minutes, trying to sort out her feelings, then put Bruce's denim jacket into her locker as carefully as if it were mink. She snatched her hand back when she caught herself stroking it as she'd once stroked the fabric of Kevin's clothes. She felt tears sting her eyes and blinked hard, closing the narrow metal door as if in doing so, she could shut up her thoughts.

She could not.

Oh, Lord, I really don't want that man in my life, she said silently. *He makes me too aware of myself, too aware of him, too aware of what I'm missing. But I'm also terribly, terribly afraid that friendship wouldn't be all I'd get, and . . .*

She paused, her hand on the door of her locker, thinking about that. Why was she so afraid? Was it fear of loving and losing again? What would she say to a patient who rejected every offer of friendship on the basis that it might turn into something more, that the "something more" might be lost and cause pain? She knew she'd counsel anyone else to take a chance, to let life happen, to accept that it wasn't always good or always fair or always what we had hoped and dreamed for, but that if we didn't reach out, didn't take a chance or two, we'd live in limbo forever.

But counseling a patient and talking sense to herself were two different things, because the fear was very real, and she knew that for all sorts of reasons, she was going to have to tread this road that beckoned with extreme care.

When Joe grinned at her as she reentered the reception room, and said, "Who's the stud, Mare?" she glared at him and said, "A neighbor," in a tone that permitted no further questions. Then they got busier and busier, and Joe, who recognized everyone's right to privacy, asked nothing more throughout their long night's work. But he did, Mary noticed, lift one gray brow when she shook her head in response to his offer to call her a taxi in the morning when their shift was nearly over.

"I'm not quite ready to go yet," she murmured, shuffling some papers on her desk, glancing out the window time and again as the hands of the clock ticked toward the half hour, feeling something inside her react with a powerful surge of happiness when a black motorcycle pulled up in front of the center at the dot of seven-thirty.

Stud felt his smile fade as he saw the lines of strain on Mary's face as she emerged from the building and crossed the sidewalk toward him. She swayed as he put her helmet on her, then without a word, she mounted the bike behind him and put her arms around him. He could feel the exhaustion in her, feel great waves of tension and sorrow and something else in her. Defeat, he thought, remembering the look in her eyes. She had looked totally defeated, and the thought bothered him.

He found himself driving very carefully, no more trying to make her hold him tighter by taking curves too fast, no more trying to get a rise out of her, no more wanting to tease. This was one whipped little doll on the back of his bike, and he suddenly wanted to take very great care of her. That surprised him, worried him, and puzzled him. What was it about her that was getting to him? Whatever it was, he'd better try to keep a curb on it, because he didn't have time for entanglements right now. Friends he wanted and needed, and something told him this little gal lacked that commodity too. He'd figured it was something they could give each other easily. But this feeling of tenderness that welled up in him each time he looked at her vulnerable face, her haunted eyes, was something to keep a damned close watch on. He, too, was vulnerable, and love was something he'd given up on finding. It would be foolish to think it could come this easy, happen so quickly.

"We're home," he said, as the engine died to a halt. "Come on, tired lady. Let's get you into bed."

"Thanks for the lift," she said, tugging the helmet off and shaking her hair loose, trying to smile. "I can get myself into bed quite nicely, thank you."

"That may be true, but you have to eat something first, and you looked too tired to go out for breakfast, so I brought you home instead. I plan to serve you breakfast in bed."

She had to laugh. "Not a chance! And I told you, I don't eat breakfast."

"Oh, yes, so you did. But today I think you should, and I think you're too tired to argue. Let's go." He wrapped an arm around her shoulder and turned her to the front doors of their apartment building. With his key, he unlocked them, and then ushered her to the elevator, right past a startled, speechless Mr. Taylor.

"Give me your key, Mary."

"I'll open the door myself," she said, refusing to relinquish her key. "Good night, Bruce. Or good morning. Whatever. Thanks again for the ride."

She unlocked her door and slipped in, closing it quickly behind her.

"Hey! Come on." He knocked loudly. "I want to do something for you!"

Lord! So much for a quiet building. He was going to wake everyone on the floor, and it was Saturday, the day most of the neighbors liked to sleep in. She opened the door a crack. "Then don't sing today, okay? Just be really, really quiet." She laughed at the expression on his face, closed the door again, and leaned on it for a moment before she dragged herself upright and staggered off to shower. She hoped he'd taken her seriously and would refrain from singing today. Too many complains, and Bruce Hagendorn would find himself evicted. For reasons she wasn't prepared to go into with herself, she didn't want that to happen.

"There once was a farmer who took a young miss . . ."

Mary sat up, rigid, eyes wide as the door to her

bedroom opened a crack, the male voice coming through loudly, followed by a foot wearing a large gray sneaker. Then a tray appeared, clutched in big brown hands, and then Bruce Hagendorn was all the way in her room. She grabbed the sheet, tugging it up over her pale pink nightgown, covering herself right up to her chin.

"In back of the barn where he gave her a lecture on—"

"What in the world are you doing in my apartment . . . in my bedroom . . . singing bawdy ballads and . . ." Words failed her, and she leaned back against the headboard, gaping at him as he set the laden tray across her lap, whipped the folded white towel from his forearm, and draped it over her bosom.

"Breakfast, m'lady. And while you eat, I'll even clean up. See how self-sacrificing I am?"

"Bruce Hagendorn, that is not self-sacrificing! That—this—is utter lunacy! How did you get in here? And *why*?"

"Because that's what friends are for." He took the key from his pocket, tossing it up and down in his hand, grinning. "I clean forgot to give this to the super, and then he went out. Saturday's his bingo day, I think he said when I was signing my lease. Hey, come on, eat up. I have to get to work, but I'm not leaving until you've finished every bite."

"Why?" she asked again. "I mean, who appointed you my caretaker?"

"Caretaker?" Head tilted to one side, he mulled that over for a bit. After a moment, he said with a nod, "I like that word," and went to lean on her dresser, one hip cocked, one foot in front of the other. "It's appropriate. For some reason, I do care about you, Mary. I want to take care of you. You had a rough night and need someone to look after you. I nominated myself, so eat, won't you? You don't want to make me late on my first day at my new job, do you?"

"I . . ." She frowned, blinking eyes that suddenly felt hot and stinging for no reason she could understand. Why should she get all tearful and emotional just because someone wanted her to eat, for heaven's sake? She didn't need anyone to care for her! It was really, really stupid, allowing Bruce Hagendorn inside her defenses like this. She could—and had—looked after herself for a long, long time, with the exception of those few years with Kevin when they had looked after each other.

She forced herself to concentrate on what he had said about his new employment. "So, you decided to take the job, did you? What is it?" she asked, to distract herself from thoughts best left in the furthest recesses of her mind.

She thought he looked a trifle shifty as he said, "I'm . . . going into business with another guy. We're old friends and rivals. He and I are ex-hockey players. He wants to expand, and I have some capital saved. We think we can work well as a team."

"What kind of business?" Mary asked with an interested smile.

He looked away. 'Oh, just a . . . business."

"I see." Okay, so he didn't want to talk about his work. She had to respect that. Maybe his reticence stemmed from his having spent too long in the public eye. *And maybe it stemmed from his being ashamed of the kind of business he was entering?* Again, she thought of those circled ads for escort services. She swallowed hard, then picked up her coffee cup and took a large gulp. She spluttered, spitting most of it back in, her nose wrinkling as she looked up at him in horror. "Holy mackerel! What is that? Sulfuric acid?"

"Too strong?" He was hurt, she could tell. "I've never made coffee with one of those filter cone things before."

"Just . . . a little strong." She took a cautious sip and set the cup down with a delicate shudder. Nope.

Not even to be polite could she drink that coffee. Not even for a man who looked like a sorrowful beagle with a black mustache, a man who wanted to be her friend, who wanted to look after her even though she didn't need that from anyone. Dammit, why did he have to be so nice? Would a guy in a shady business be genuinely nice? Would a genuinely nice guy enter a shady business? And were all escort services shady? She knew they weren't, but . . .

She took a bite of the scrambled eggs, chewed, swallowed, and then smiled. "The eggs are good."

"Try the bacon," he said eagerly, beaming as he crossed his arms over his shirtfront, showing off his impressive shoulders and forearms. Obviously, he'd forgotten his offer to clean up while she ate.

"It's great too," she said, nibbling a piece, then laying three strips of it on half a slice of toast and covering it with another triangle of toast. She munched her sandwich.

"Well, look at you," he said, clearly delighted. "I do that, too, you know. Make sandwiches out of my toast and bacon. Next time would you like a cheese-and-bacon sandwich? Or a fried egg sandwich with bacon? Or bacon and tomato? I'm pretty good with sandwiches. I even make one that is superdelicious, but I can't talk anyone else into trying it. French fries and ketchup on rye bread with lots of mayonnaise and raw onions."

Mary stared at him, not sure he was serious. But somebody had to be serious here, didn't they?

"Bruce . . . there can't be a next time. I'm really grateful for this," she waved a hand over the tray, not quite including the coffee, "but you can't just wander in and out of my apartment, you know."

"I know." He looked contrite. "And I won't do it again unless I'm invited. It was just that I'd promised you breakfast this morning, and I didn't want you to feel cheated because you were too tired to go out for it. I owed you."

He didn't, of course, because she hadn't really expected him to be there in spite of his having said he would. "Thank you."

What else, she wondered, could she possibly say? Especially around that damned big lump in her throat. She didn't want to let his kindness touch her, but she couldn't help it. She didn't want him acting as if she were unable to look after herself, because it would be so easy to permit him to do it now and again, until he'd taken over completely. She hadn't wanted him to, would have hated it if he'd tried. But just now . . . She knew she was tired of being alone all the time; she had to admit that, and if he wormed his way into her life, his affection could weaken her, steal her strengths, those strengths she needed in order to get through each day, each night, each year of her future. She'd worked long and hard to build that core of discipline within herself, to control her emotions, to disallow any need for closeness lest it overshadow the essential toughness of her spirit.

Some had referred to what she'd built as a shell, but it wasn't that, nor was it a pretense. It was solid, strong, and very necessary to her survival. It was her spine. And this man seemed to have some kind of magic solvent that threatened to destroy it, sending her caving in under the weight of needs and desires and wants she had buried long ago.

"I was worried about you," he went on. "It was a real rough night, huh?"

"Huh," she said in dry agreement. One old man had died before the ambulance came to take him to the hospital for treatment the center wasn't equipped to offer. Died screaming. It had not been pretty. Yet, until Bruce Hagendorn had showed up on his trusty mechanized steed, lance at the ready to slay her dragons, she hadn't even been aware that dragons were lurking in the memories of the night which had been like so many other nights before it.

He sat down on the chair under the window, spread his knees, and leaned his arms on them. "What happened?"

She shrugged and swallowed another bite of egg. "Just the usual. The cops brought in a few drunks who needed help. So we helped them."

"And hated it."

She frowned, but said nothing. How could he possibly know how much she had come to hate it these past few months? What was he, some kind of wizard?

"What bothers you most about the work you do?"

"Hey, who's the psychologist here, you or me?" She tried desperately to inject a little lightness into a conversation that was getting far too heavy.

"I'm not trying to be a psychologist, Mary. I'm just trying to be your friend. Can't you talk to me about it?"

She drew in a tremulous breath. Maybe it would help to talk about it. Maybe that would release some of the pressure. Last night over dinner she'd talked to him, and, oddly, it had increased her strength to face the night ahead. Letting out her breath, she said, "It bothers me every time I have to help someone who's seeing little black bugs on the walls, or is fighting off terrifying threats like . . . like . . ." She cast her mind back to the night before, remembering the screams. "Like umbrellas only he can see, or snakes or whatever. It bothers me to see the same faces returning again and again. It bothers me to think that no matter what we do, it's never enough, because we can't change a damned thing about the real reasons for our having to be there: Poverty, apathy, alcoholism and—" She broke off with a sheepish little laugh and blew her hair off her brow with a little puff of air. She clenched her teeth, swallowed hard, and then unclenched her fists with a conscious effort, smoothing her hands over her satin bedspread.

"Sorry. I was about to go into my favorite spiel

again. After four years you'd think I'd be used to it, but I'm not."

"Why don't you quit?" he asked softly. "It's too hard on you, I can tell."

After a moment she added, "I don't intend to spend the rest of my life working there. When I've earned my doctorate, I want to work with teenagers. But right now I need the center as much as it needs me. I'm doing my thesis on the correlation of family position and alcoholism."

"Family position? You mean rich, poor, leaders in the community or . . . what?"

"No. None of that. Personal placement in the family. Eldest, youngest, middle, one of a large family, one of a small family, and so on. Part of my job is to interview our patients, counsel them, help them to understand why they drink so that maybe they can find a way to quit. I can get a lot of the information I need doing that, even though it's painful having to deal with the problems they have. And like I said before, someone needs to care about them."

"It's a very hard job to do, isn't it? Aren't there other sources you could use to get the material you need for your thesis?"

"Yes. Of course. And I do use other sources, but the stories I hear are just as awful no matter where I hear them. A drunk is a drunk, whether it's an old man on skid road or a polite housewife from South Granville. But my work at the center is important. I like to think that maybe I do help a little."

"And maybe you help a lot," he suggested.

"I don't know." Again he was aware of the look of defeat in her eyes. "What would help would be people never getting to that stage in the first place."

"Aren't you working at the wrong end of the business then, if that's what you'd like to see?"

She nodded. "But like I said, I don't intend to be there forever. I want to work with kids, maybe prevent their getting to that stage, or nipping a problem at its very inception. So much of it starts in childhood, you know, dependency on drugs and alcohol. Some start drinking or taking drugs because of work or social pressures at home or at school, others from good old-fashioned peer pressure. One of the biggest problems is that kids have no places to go where they can hang out with other kids and not be tempted by things that are bad for them. There's a common belief among young people today that they *cannot* have a good time unless they are drunk or stoned. This is reinforced daily by their parents, who come home from work, have a drink to 'relax,' then go out to the local bar with their friends for a 'fun' evening. Kids learn to equate fun with booze almost from the cradle, so you can't blame them, and by the time they're alcoholic adults, many of them simply can't be helped adequately."

"Why not?" He looked thoughtful sitting there, leaning his forearms on his thighs.

She really didn't want to talk about it, but there was something compelling in his face. "If we had the answer to that, we'd have alcoholism licked. But recidivism is one of the biggest problems. The patients we got last night, like those who came in before, well, we'll dry them out, counsel them, try to help them find out why they live the way they do, try to turn them around, try to help them. And then we'll discharge them because we have to, because we need room for others in worse shape, and at least they're sober for the time being. And each one we release has no place to go except back to his grubby rooming house or hotel, where there's nothing to do but wait for Welfare Wednesday once a month because he has no job, no family. So he'll drink and make himself ill again and come back to us, if he doesn't die on some corner or in an alley first. They have no hope anymore, most of the people down there. It just goes on and on endlessly, and I think sometimes what I'm doing is of no value because we win out against the bugbears so very, very seldom."

"But you do win?" he asked gently, leaning farther forward as he looked into her eyes, sharing her misery, wanting to alleviate it somehow. "What constitutes a victory, Mary?"

She thought about that. One way to look at last night's death was as a victory, she supposed. At least old Charlie wouldn't be back. And maybe, though at times she doubted it, he'd gone on to someplace better.

"Oh, yes, sometimes we win," she admitted finally. "Rarely, though. Joe, a fellow who works with me, is one success story we're all proud of. He used to be one of them, in and out of one or another of the detoxes, but he's all dried out now and been sober for two years. He's dedicated his life to working to help others. And he can really understand where they're coming from having lived it himself."

"Then you know there's hope."

After a moment, she smiled. She had to. He was right. Of course there was hope, or she wouldn't be doing what she did. "Sure, there's hope. Some. Sorry, it just gets to me sometimes, and I come close to giving up."

"How about I put some hot water in that coffee for you?" he asked, getting to his feet.

"Sure," she said. "But how about just putting a little bit of this coffee into some hot water?"

He grinned, and when he returned with a decent cup of coffee, she took a sip and thanked him. "It's nearly five o'clock," he said. "I have to go to work. Can I pick you up again in the morning? Same time, same place?"

"What time will you get off work?"

He shrugged. "In time to come and get you."

"Why do I suddenly think you're being cagey? What time, Bruce?"

He pulled a face. "You sound like my tenth-grade

science teacher," he said. "Only she used to say, 'The answer, Bruce,' in exactly the same tone of voice while she fixed me with her evil eye."

Mary narrowed her gaze on him, trying to look evil. "The answer, Bruce."

"You'll never make it as a science teacher." He chuckled. "All right. I'll get home about two-thirty or three. But I can easily grab a few hours sleep and then come for you."

"No. Absolutely not."

What kind of a job has hours like that? She wanted to ask him but kept her mouth shut because the first one that came to mind was escort service, of course, and she didn't want to know about that. Her dismay made her feel sick. Was he really going into partnership with a friend who ran one of those? Was he going to work in the office or take a more active role? Though it was mostly women in demand as escorts, she knew there were men doing the same job, providing company for visiting businesswomen who didn't like to dine alone. Or whatever. While there might be legitimate escort services, she suspected that most of them were fronts for other more intimate "services."

She frowned. For a man who seemed to see himself in the role of a caregiver, as well as a stud, it might just be the ideal job. She shook herself mentally. It was none of her cotton-pickin' business what he did with his life!

He clearly didn't feel the same way about her. "I don't like the idea of your taking a bus out of that area at that time of day any more than I liked the idea of your going there yesterday evening, or this evening."

"I take a taxi to and from work," she said, "unless there's a pushy ex-hockey player revving up his bike beside me. Really, the foundation that runs the center pays for my taxis, so it's not a problem. Please, don't come for me in the morning." Seeing him begin to look stubborn, she turned on her own obstinate switch. "If you do, I won't ride with you, so why waste your sleeping hours that way? You'll have to work the next night, won't you?"

"No. I won't be working on Sunday or Monday."

She drew in a deep breath. "What do you do, Bruce? I've told you about my job. Why don't you tell me about yours?"

His face went blank all of a sudden, confirming her worst suspicions. "I will," he said with a quick smile. "Another time. Gotta run." He flipped her spare key onto her bed, bent swiftly, and covered her surprised lips with his. As kisses went, it was brief. And coming from someone who answered to the nickname Stud, it was not very expert, mostly missing her mouth and bouncing off her chin. But it shook her as she'd never been shaken before, setting up a clamor inside her that demanded more and more.

For several moments after he was gone, she just sat there, staring into space, remembering the way he had smelled, the way he had tasted, the way he had felt—but most of all the way his kiss had made her feel, all warm and mushy and soft inside. She lifted one hand and touched her lips with her fingertips, feeling the shape of the smile he had left on them. They quivered, and she quickly dropped her hand. She set the tray aside and slithered back down under her covers, reviewing the past half hour with amazement.

What was the matter with her, letting a perfect stranger into her bedroom without screaming the place down or even reaching for the phone at her bedside and dialing 911? Letting him serve her a meal she hadn't really wanted, although she noticed she'd eaten every bite. Letting him force her to talk about things she never discussed with anyone? Letting him kiss her? Oh, dammit, she was out of her mind! Of course she was! That would account for her almost irrepressible urge to laugh aloud and dance around the room.

But when she finally got up and surveyed the incredible mess in her kitchen, she didn't feel like dancing or laughing, and began to understand exactly why the man didn't like cleaning up after himself. He was a slob and had dirtied every dish in the kitchen, dribbled eggs across the stove, splattered bacon grease over everything, and strewn toast crumbs across every flat surface there was. Next time, she told herself, she'd make sure he did what he'd promised, even if it meant standing over him with a two-by-four in her hand. But . . . wait a minute! There wasn't going to be a next time. Hadn't she told him that? Of course she had.

Now the only one she had to convince was herself.

Bruce Hagendorn was a stranger, and he wasn't getting into her apartment again. She sighed as she started loading the dishwasher. For some reason he didn't seem in the least like a stranger, and she wasn't at all sure she wanted to keep him out.

Four

When the knock came on her door Sunday afternoon, Mary was immersed in a fat tome dealing with
the intricacies of fetal alcohol syndrome. She brought
herself back to the world around her with difficulty
and went to the door, opening it just a crack with
the chain still on.

It was Bruce, wearing jeans and a half-buttoned
gray shirt. "You busy?"

"Yes," she said. "I'm studying. Just a minute,
okay?" She shut the door, unfastened the chain,
and opened the door again, leaning on the door
frame, smiling but not inviting him in. Her heart
and other portions of her anatomy were acting in
strange ways. The more she saw this man, the more
he affected her. She wasn't certain she liked it, but,
on reflection, what was there not to like? Except for
the way he earned his living, of course.

Bruce returned her smile, watching with interest
the play of emotions on her face, the way color came
and went like fluttering flags on her cheekbones. It
was all he could do not to grab her and run away to
his apartment—a caveman dragging home his chosen morsel.

"What can I do for you?" she asked, and he was hard put not to tell her.

"I came to apologize," he said, instead of mouthing off with the truth. "I forgot to clean up your kitchen yesterday. Can I make amends by taking you out for dinner?"

She looked momentarily wistful, he thought, but shook her head. "I have too much to do."

"Hey, come on. You have to eat. It'll be quicker to go out for a bite than it will be stopping work long enough to cook."

"It's quicker for me to have a bowl of soup and a sandwich than it is to get dressed, go out, wait to get served, then eat and come home again."

He sighed, nodded, and left, and Mary went back to work, forcing herself to concentrate, but only for about five minutes. Her mind refused to stick with her studies; instead, it conjured up pictures of a man with a drooping mustache walking away down the hall toward the stairs, his shoulders also drooping, his feet dragging. Lonesome, alone in a strange city, no friends. She felt guilty and churlish and mean. Dammit, why did she let him get to her? If he was lonely, why didn't he join a health club or something, go to a singles' bar, do whatever lonely people in strange places did.

Hire an escort service. Or hire on with one.

Deliberately and with difficulty she put the man out of her mind and continued reading. Or tried to. Presently, realizing it was futile to try to work while her mind was filled with the memory of the sound of a certain male voice, she made herself the soup and sandwich she'd mentioned and took them out onto the balcony with a term paper from last year for company, hoping she might be able to utilize some of the information she'd researched then. She had just sat down, just taken her first mouthful of cream of mushroom soup, when he spoke.

"What are you reading?"

She started, lifted her head, and looked one suite over and one floor down. Bruce, lolling in his wading pool, hands laced behind his neck, was looking up at her. He had a can of beer beside him. She told him, and he tsk-tsked disapprovingly. "It's bad for your digestion, working while you eat. Why don't you read a nice romantic story to get you in the mood?"

Her brows lifted. "In the mood for what?"

"For going to a movie with me tonight after you finish studying."

"But I'm not going to a movie with you tonight after I finish studying. I'm going to bed."

He lifted his head expectantly, a smile on his lips, a devilish glint in his eyes. "Sounds good to me. What time?"

"All by myself," she told him, fighting the urge to laugh at and with him, "and probably no later than ten o'clock." She could only hope that the people above her weren't out on their patio listening to this crazy conversation.

He sighed. "Some friend you're turning out to be. I'm lonely, Mary. You're the only person I know here, besides my partner, and he's busy with his wife and three kids. He invited me to take potluck with them, but frankly, charred hot dogs don't appeal to me. If you don't want to have dinner with me, or go to a movie, how about a walk on the beach?"

Something hurtful stabbed her inside where she was softest, where even the stoutest core had tiny chinks. A walk on the beach? For a moment a vision flickered in her mind: Kevin running on the wet sand at the water's edge. Andy, feet splashing, leaping up and down in the ripples, his face alight with laughter. Herself between them, loving them both so much she ached with it, not feeling any of the sense of foreboding she'd told herself over and over again she *should* have felt. If they'd left the beach one minute earlier, one minute later . . . For the first time in a long while she felt the old, deep and almost irrepressible need to scream building within her.

"Mary?" The concern in Bruce's tone brought her out of her momentary remembrance. He got to his feet, standing ankle-deep in water, frowning up at her. "You okay?"

She blinked away the past and its horrors and focused on Bruce, the present. "Yes. Of course."

"Then what was it? What were you thinking about?"

"Nothing, really," she said, fighting hard against the pain the memory had brought. "Just . . . maybe you should join some kind of a group, make some friends." She cast frantically back to what she had decided earlier would be his best course of action. "What about a health club? You'd even get the use of a swimming pool."

He grinned and swirled one foot around. "You don't approve of my wading pool?"

"I didn't say that."

"But you look disapproving. I find my pool relaxing. Especially when I play my ocean tape."

"You're not playing it now. Maybe you should."

"When I do, I usually sing. I don't want to bother any of the neighbors." He grinned, and she knew she was the only neighbor he was worried about bothering. Only he wasn't worried enough about it to go away and leave her to eat her soup and sandwich in peace. She lifted another spoonful of soup. It was cold. She looked at her sandwich. Cucumber and sprouts on five-grain bread didn't seem as appealing as it had half an hour ago.

She set her spoon down and shoved her bowl and plate to the other side of the table.

"Eat," he said, stepping out of the pool and leaning on the rail of his balcony, looking up at her intently. Through the clear Plexiglas panels she could see his wet trunks and beads of water running through the hair on his thighs. Oddly her own thighs tickled as if the water were trickling over her skin.

"No. It doesn't taste very good."

"What would taste good?"

The question surprised her, but what surprised her more was that the answer popped into her mind at the same instant it popped from her mouth. "Chinese food."

"Sounds great to me. Order in, or go out?"

"I . . . I'm not doing either. I have to study."

"You have to eat," he said. "Get changed. I'll be up there in ten minutes. If you're not there to open your door, I'll tell Mr. Taylor you're sick and need my help. He'll give me the key."

"He will not! I'll call him right now and tell him you're going to come telling lies about me and . . ." But she was talking to thin air and a half-filled green wading pool. Dammit, why couldn't the man have ordinary patio furniture like everyone else? A wading pool, for heaven's sake. How could anyone take him seriously?

And why did she want to?

She was dressed and waiting when he knocked on her door, and without a word he tucked her hand into the crook of his elbow, smiled at her, and limped to the elevator. She was about to ask if he'd hurt himself, when she noticed he had on only one shoe. The other, she saw, was jammed in the door of the elevator, holding it in position for them.

"That," she said disapprovingly, "could get you evicted, you know."

"Nah . . . Jerry likes me. I gave him autographs for his grandkids."

"Jerry?"

"Jerry Taylor."

Mary blinked. Nobody, but nobody, called Mr. Taylor anything but Mr. Taylor. That was how he introduced himself to every new tenant when he was busy laying down the law about how things would be done: Garbage packaged in just such a manner; cars parked only in designated slots; visitors out by a certain time; subleases not permitted at all. That he was Mr. Taylor and would be addressed as such was only implicit, but still very clear. It was the way he signed notes if he had to leave them. And here was this man, having lived there only a week or two, already on first-name terms with the super. "I didn't know he had grandchildren." She didn't even know he'd ever been married.

"Sure. Seven of them. All boys. His youngest son's wife is pregnant again, and they're hoping for a girl. Jerry's wife always yearned for a little girl, but all they had were four sons. She died six years ago. He watches the soaps and game shows she used to watch so that when he meets up with her again in heaven, he can tell her who's doing what."

Mary gaped, and he lifted his hand to close her mouth before putting the red helmet on her. For the first time she realized that they were outside in the warm evening air with the sound of birdsong all around and the sun sinking toward Vancouver Island, turning the air to living gold.

She looked up at Bruce Hagendorn in the clear, golden light and said bemusedly, "How did you do this? I don't ever remember saying yes."

He met her gaze. "Oh, you didn't." He cupped her chin with one hand and looked at her a bit longer, then brushed his mouth over hers. "But you're going to, Mary. One of these days. Of that I'm absolutely certain."

She returned his solemn gaze for several moments, wanting to tell him that he hadn't asked a question yet, but she saw in his eyes that he had, and that he was willing to wait for her reply.

She shivered in spite of the warmth, then sighed softly and moved away from him, feeling bewildered and bemused and bewitched, and suddenly very light-headed. She wondered about the smile that curved her mouth and refused to leave as she ducked her head down against his back and felt the powerful machine take them flying away. In spite of herself, she laughed.

He was some man, this Hagendorn stud!

"How the heck do you do that so easily?"

Mary held her chopsticks loosely so Bruce could see the placement of her fingers. "Relax your hand," she said, setting hers down so she could guide the sticks in his grip. "There, now you've got it. The control is in your middle finger. No, don't try to pick up too much at one time."

"I'll starve to death feeding myself one grain of rice every thirty seconds," he complained.

"You can use your fork," she said.

He looked around the crowded, noisy restaurant. Mary hadn't brought him to a place frequented by Caucasians. She'd insisted the food would be better here in this small, out-of-the-way corner on Powell Street, where ninety-nine percent of the diners were Oriental. It was, he'd noticed, very close to the detox center where she worked.

The waiter had addressed Mary by name, smiled, and spoken to her in such high-pitched, rapid, fractured English that Stud hadn't been able to make out one word in five. But the food she and the old Chinese man had chosen for them was the best he'd ever eaten, or would be, he was sure, if he could just eat it. The aromas were driving him into such hunger spasms, he was almost ready to drop the chopsticks and dip his fingers into that bowl of steaming noodles. All he'd had so far was an incredible soup which he'd eaten with a little china spoon and an egg roll which he'd picked up in his fingers.

"I'd be ashamed to eat with a fork," he said. "No

one else here is using one. No one else here even has one." Nor, he heard, was anyone else even speaking English. He struggled, then held out his hand to her. "Help me again."

Several times during the meal she repositioned his chopsticks for him before she caught on that he was only using his ineptitude as an excuse to make her touch him.

"You really are a brat," she said, grinning in spite of herself.

"That's what my mom tells me. I ask her whose fault that is, who raised me, and she says, 'Your dad and your grandmother.' "

"Are you close to your family? Don't you miss them, being so far from home?"

He nodded. "Yes, to both. I come from a big family. Three brothers, two sisters, one of whom is my twin." He smiled, as if thinking loving thoughts. She was envious. How different would her life have been if she'd had family to turn to when she was in such great need? "Tracy," he added, naming his twin.

"Where do you and Tracy fit?"

"Hey, now, none of that. We aren't alcoholics."

"That's not why I asked!"

He laughed at her look of consternation and relented. "I know that, and I was only teasing. We'e in the middle. Jason and Paul are older than we are, Maggie and Phil are younger."

"Does she look like you? Your twin?"

"Well . . . She doesn't have a mustache."

Mary laughed, and his eyes twinkled as he continued. "She doesn't look like me in the least. She's little and blond and cute as a button. She's even shorter than you are."

"I'm not short at all. I'm five four."

He grinned. "And I'm six four. That, sweet Mary, makes you short by comparison."

There wasn't a lot of argument to that. "My dad

always says I got stretched from leaning out, reaching for the puck," Bruce went on. "I'm the tallest of the tribe."

"How long did you play hockey?"

"Too long. I started in a peewee league when I was about eighteen months old. At least that's when they put me on skates. Before my asthma was brought under control, I was usually too laid up in summer to do many sports, so my family really had me concentrate on hockey. Sometimes it seems my entire life was school and hockey games and hockey clinics."

"Did you like it?"

He hesitated. "Yeah, I guess so. It was what I could do best, and at least all those years of fooling around on the ice paid off."

"Not everyone who spends his childhood 'fooling around on the ice' ends up with an NHL berth," she said. "I'm sure your family feels great pride in your accomplishments."

"Ending up in the NHL was pure luck. Right place at the right time," he said with a shrug. "I played professionally for eighteen years. Lots of guys play much longer."

So he didn't want to admit that superior skill had put him where he'd been. "Do you miss it?"

He was thoughtful for several minutes, managing to get a few more bites of food down. "Yes and no. I miss being part of a team. The team was always important to me, never doing anything that we hadn't figured out as a group, planning strategy, getting things all sorted out so that we knew what to do and when to do it, even in the excitement of the game. And there was the camaraderie of the other guys, too, the after-game bashes." He smiled. "We always partied, win or lose."

"You like parties a lot?" she asked.

He nodded. "I love having lots of people around me, and music and laughter and activity. Fun times. Comes of being part of a big family, I guess, all close together in age, all of us gregarious as hell. Things are never quiet at home," he added wistfully.

Mary felt a momentary sadness. She and Bruce were so very different. She found parties mostly boring. It wasn't much fun watching strangers drink themselves silly. Of course, there were parties and then there were parties. She and Kevin used to attend some good ones, and even gave the odd one, and she sometimes enjoyed the ones Aggie and Steve put on. But mostly she avoided them.

"So it's not just hockey you miss, but your family, your friends, the good times you had with them."

He nodded. "Yes to all of that, but one thing I don't miss is the injuries, the aches and pains that got worse every winter after I turned thirty." He narrowed his gaze at her, then lifted one brow. "You there yet?"

She shook her head. "Next November."

"Well, I hit that mark over six years ago. Believe me, it's no myth. After thirty you heal slower, things hurt worse, your body isn't what it used to be at eighteen or twenty-two, or even twenty-five. This"—he fingered his mustache—"hides a scar that I got as a young kid, and that was one of the few injuries I ever suffered early on." He rubbed the bridge of his nose. "This old schnozz was busted five times, three of them after I hit the big three-oh. My left leg has two healed fractures, my right, one, and both my shoulders have been dislocated a few times as well. I figured it out finally: I was getting too slow. Even if others played until they were old and gray, that wasn't for me."

"And so you quit. I heard you retired two years—" She broke off, chagrined to have him know she'd been talking about him, asking questions.

He didn't seem to mind, or maybe he thought she just shared the general knowledge of the rest of the world. "That's right, I did."

"What did you do . . . after you retired, I mean, before you came here?"

He shrugged. "This and that."

"In Winnipeg?"

"Near there. I worked on the farm with my family part of the time, when they needed me. Hung out with my friends. Partied a lot. Spent money."

"And then came out here."

He set down his chopsticks. "And then came out here." He sipped his green tea, holding the little handleless cup in both hands, avoiding her gaze.

"Why?" She challenged him deliberately. They both knew it.

He looked up from under drawn brows. "Why not?"

"Because you're a self-confessed party-hound who needs people and music and laughter and fun. You like to have your friends around you, and your family. Why come to a place where you don't know anybody?"

He smiled and shrugged again. "You know the answer to that, shrink."

"I'm no shrink, Bruce, but I can read between the lines . . . friend," she said gently, a little smile on her mouth, compassion in her eyes as she looked at his moody face. "What's her name? What happened?"

"Her name's Evelyn, and she's my youngest sister's best friend. She boards with our family. We dated for a while, had a few laughs." He fiddled with his chopsticks, poked them into his leftovers, then dropped them with a clatter. He met Mary's gaze, his eyes troubled.

"She suddenly changed the rules in the middle of the game. She fell in love with me. She said since I hadn't dated anyone else since I'd started taking her out, she thought I felt the same way. She wanted to get married, make babies with me. Get our own little farm or something. That wasn't what I wanted. It wasn't in my game plan at all. I was hurting her by staying around. So I left."

"And your family?"

"My family's not very happy with me right now."

She frowned. "They wanted you to marry someone you didn't love?"

"No," he said. "They're not that unreasonable. What they wanted was for me to love her. And I didn't. I can't. I didn't want to hurt her!" he added miserably. "I never gave her any reason to believe that what we were sharing was anything more than just . . ."

"A few laughs."

He looked uncomfortable at her offering his own words back to him, but he had to admit they were true. "Well, yes. I mean, she's a grown woman. She's twenty-six. She's nice and I like her a lot. She's an elementary school teacher, bright, witty, sophisticated, great to talk to and great in—" He broke off with a grimace, ducking his head down. He picked up a crumb from an egg roll and nibbled it. Looking up again, he said, "What I felt for Evelyn simply wasn't . . . forever, and if that makes me the rat my little sister Maggie called me, then I guess I'm a rat."

"Or a man with too much integrity to be pressured by his family into marrying someone he doesn't love. I don't suppose it was easy, breaking it off with her, moving away, all that."

He looked stunned. "You're the first person to see it that way, Mary. Thanks." His gaze sharpened. "But you still disapprove of me, don't you? Of the way I handled things with Evelyn."

"No," she said quickly, shaking her head. "Maybe it was wrong of you to date someone exclusively, if you didn't mean anything by it, but as you said, she's an adult. If you didn't make any promises, then she shouldn't have expected you to be there forever."

"I can still read censure in your pretty blue eyes, though," he said. "What is it that bothers you?"

He could, she thought, read altogether too much

when he looked at her. Why did she lose her poker face when he was around? Or was it simply that he was capable of seeing through it? "I have a hard time dealing with the idea of a thirty-six-year-old man who thinks all there is to life is parties and fun."

"That's blunt and to the point. Do you see me on a little farm somewhere in Manitoba, growing wheat or whatever? Don't you know that little farms aren't economical anymore?"

"I don't see you anywhere in particular. But doing something productive, yes. I think that's a necessity for any mature adult, for self-esteem, personal growth."

"I am doing something productive," he said. "I'm a businessman, remember? I have a partnership with another guy, and I think we'll do well working as a team."

"But clearly it's not the kind of business you can share with Evelyn." *Or even tell a friend about.* Yet, his friend and new partner, according to Bruce, had a wife and three children. She wondered if the friend's wife knew the truth about what the business was. And if so, how did she feel about it?

"It's not my *business* I don't want to share with her. It's my *life.*"

So. He was just another of those modern men who didn't want to make a commitment. Well, it was his life. "Yes, of course. I'm sorry. It's none of my concern anyway. I didn't mean to look disapproving."

She bent and picked up her helmet off the floor, then got to her feet. "We really should go home. I've spent far longer away from my books than I meant to."

"We haven't got our bill yet."

"Mr. Leung will have it waiting at the cash register for us," she assured him, and let him take her hand as they walked between the crowded tables. She smiled and nodded at a few familiar faces, spoke soft greetings here and there, and when they got to the desk at the front of the long, narrow room, reached for the bill Mr. Leung held ready.

Offended, Stud snatched it out of her hand, glanced at it, then stared. "One dollar and sixty cents? Look, there's some kind of mis—"

"Hush," said Mary, squeezing his fingers tightly, her eyes sending him some kind of warning. "Are you going to pay it, or will you give it back to me so I can?"

"But it's wrong and—"

Mary smacked one dollar, two quarters, and a dime onto the counter, said thanks and good night to Mr. Leung, and towed her unwilling companion outside.

"I can't believe you'd cheat that nice old man that way! He made a mistake, Mary! What if he loses his job over it? Why wouldn't you let me point it out to him?"

"It was no mistake, and he's the owner of the restaurant, so he can't lose his job. He's my friend. He lets me pay for the tea. That's the compromise we reached that allows both of us to save face. If I don't go there for lunch or dinner at least once each month, he comes looking for me at the center to make sure I'm all right, and drags me around the corner for a good meal. So I make a habit of eating here just often enough to keep him happy but not so often as to become a financial drain."

"Why?"

"Why what?" She knew perfectly well what Bruce was asking.

"What does he owe you for?"

"Nothing," she said with a deprecating shrug. "But he thinks he does. His grandson was in . . . trouble. I talked to him a few times is all, helped him sort himself out."

Trouble? Stud wondered just what kind of trouble the boy had been in for his grandfather to have gone for help from someone who worked in a detox center. It didn't take a lot of imagination to figure that one out.

"That's what you want to do with your life, isn't it?" he asked. "Work with addicted teens. Why aren't you doing it now?"

She sighed. "Unfortunately, there aren't very many places that deal with kids' addiction problems just yet. But that will change. It's going to have to," she added, and bit her lip, thinking about all the young people who needed help and weren't getting it. Governments worked so slowly!

"Kids are notoriously hard to reach, though, aren't they?" asked Bruce, looping the strap of his helmet over the handlebar of the bike and leaning back against the seat, arms folded, looking at her with interest. "How do you get through to them?"

"The same way you get through to anyone else," she said. "Earn their trust; prove that you truly care what happens to them. Take Mr. Leung's grandson, for instance. Without breaking any codes of ethics I can tell you that he'd just gotten off the track somewhere. For a variety of reasons he'd lost his belief in himself, felt that he wasn't performing in a manner that pleased his family, and that no matter what he did, it wasn't good enough. Therefore, as he saw it, there was no point in even trying anymore. He got mixed up with the wrong crowd. All I did was talk to him and help him see that he had a lot going for him. Sort of rebuilt his confidence, patched up his bruised self-esteem."

"I have a feeling there was a lot more to it than that," said Stud.

Mary shrugged. "No matter. He's straight and clean now, and a credit to himself and his family."

Bruce came erect and stood over her, looking serious. "You must feel such pride in what you do."

She met his gaze. "Sometimes," she said. "Yes." She fought down the feelings that surged up in her. *He* was proud of her! In effect that was what he'd just said, and it was wonderful to hear it. She drew in a shuddering breath and half-turned from him, shifting her helmet to her other hand, keeping it almost as a shield between them.

He went to take it from her, but she lifted it herself and tugged it on, buckling her own strap so that he wouldn't have to do it for her. She didn't want him to touch her throat, her neck, her hair. Oh, who was she kidding? The trouble was, she *did* want him to do all that and more, but it was better for her if she prevented such things from happening.

When she had it securely fastened, he clasped the helmet in both hands and tilted her face up, looking deeply into her eyes. "I used to feel pride in a game well played," he said, "but somehow, I don't think it's quite the same. Here you are quietly putting lives back together, fixing up broken people, earning the respect and gratitude of their families."

She forced a small laugh. "Don't be so serious about all this," she chided him. Serious was not what she'd come to expect of him. It threw her off balance. "You earned a lot of respect as a sports figure," she reminded him, "and possibly even the gratitude of those who put money on your team."

He knocked on the side of her helmet with his knuckles. "That's not the same," he said. "And I think you know it. You work. I play."

"And speaking of work," she said, "you have to take me home now. I still have a lot to do." She wasn't about to get into a discussion of personal worth with him right here and now, but if he were feeling guilty about his partnership in an escort service, then all well and good. Yet . . . it was still only speculation on her part that that was what he did, she reminded herself.

At her door he stood looking down at her. "I don't suppose I could persuade you to play a little longer?"

She laughed. "You and your playing! Some people

can't play all the time, you know. There are toilers, and there are lilies of the field. Good night, lily."

He grinned. "That's even more of a sissy name than Bruce. You know what, Mary DeLaney?" He stepped closer so that their bodies were within centimeters of touching.

A slow, heavy throbbing began deep inside her. "What?" she asked, in little more than a whisper.

"I'm going to have to kiss you good night."

"Oh." Several heartbeats passed before she could continue. "Why . . . 'have to'?" Didn't he want to? As much as she wanted to kiss him?

"Because we've just come back from a date. Our first real date. I asked you out, and you agreed." She could have argued that point, but he was continuing. "And I want you to go to sleep tonight thinking of Stud, not Lily."

Again she laughed, and in that moment he captured her mouth in a sweet, wild kiss that turned her inside out, left her with shining eyes and parted lips and a heart flying in crazy patterns inside her chest. Slowly his hands left her shoulders, trailing down her arms to the tips of her fingers. Slowly he backed away from her.

He looks, she thought, *exactly the way I feel. Spaced-out, befuddled, and unsure if the feelings are good or bad.*

"Good night," she murmured, still looking at him.

"Yeah." He backed away another pace or two.

He paused at the end of the corridor with his hand on the door leading to the stairs. "Go inside, Mary," he said in a loud whisper.

"I will."

"Now. Before I leave. So I can go knowing you're safely locked in."

She unlocked her door, opened it, then turned and smiled. "Bruce?"

"What?" His voice was gruff.

"I'm glad you're my friend." And then she closed

her door softly. He pictured her leaning against the inside of it as weak-kneed as he was, just as shaken by that incredible little kiss and just as shocked by the feelings it had generated.

Friend? Did she still just want to be his friend?

And if she did, what chance did he have of retaining her friendship once he told her the truth about his new business venture?

Five

Bruce left her to her studies for the next several days, and Mary tried hard to tell herself she was not disappointed, but inside she ached for the sight and sound of him, the feel of his mouth on hers, the scent of his skin. Those few little teasing brushes of his mouth over hers had not been enough. Nor had that one real kiss done anything to still the growing hunger in her blood. How, in so few days, had the man gotten under her skin so deeply? Each evening she swore she was putting him out of her mind, and while she worked, she was often successful for several hours at a time, but then . . . then she had to sleep, and the man had the sneaky habit of infiltrating her dreams.

Vacation's coming up, she told herself repeatedly. *I'll go away.* But where could she go? Solitary vacations were the pits. While Kevin's parents frequently invited her to visit them in Kelowna, she normally refused; it was too painful to be in the house where he'd grown up, to sleep in the room he'd had as a boy and young man, to see pictures of him and Andy all over. His parents had their way of dealing with loss and grief, but it was not her way. All those pictures hurt. Still, maybe this time she'd do it. Maybe it was time she had a stern reminder. She was not looking for a relationship with any man!

It was hard to remember that, though, when she arrived home on Tuesday afternoon and saw Bruce coming out the front doors, dressed in a dark suit, a blue-and-green-patterned tie, and shiny shoes. He was gorgeous, and something caught in her chest, expanded until it hurt, then exploded, leaving her feeling weak and dizzy. He hadn't spotted her yet, and she let herself drink in the sight of his long, loose-limbed stride, the jaunty way he bounded down the four steps to the parking area, the slight tilt of his head, the way the sun caught in his dark hair and burnished it. He passed through the shadow of a Lombardy poplar, then moved back out into the light again, and she saw him come to a halt as he caught sight of her.

Stud felt his heart slam to a stop as Mary came walking down the sidewalk from the bus stop. She had her books under her arm and was squinting into the angled sun, a smile on her face that he knew was all for him as she swung into the driveway, full cotton skirt playing around her knees in a pink froth. His breath did something strange inside his chest, and he hurried to meet her, an answering smile on his face. It had been altogether too long since he'd seen her, spoken to her, and while he'd been damn busy these past few days, his nights had been long and lonely. He wanted to spend a lot more time with this woman. And not just for sex, either, he recognized with another jolt. He'd missed talking to Mary, listening to her, looking at her. But most of all, he'd missed touching her. Funny, he'd known her such a short time, but the feel of her skin was like an addiction. He wanted more and more.

Mary just barely managed not to quiver when he touched her. "Hi," he said, sliding one hand up her arm onto her shoulder, leaving it to lie there like a warm blanket, one long finger just under the edge of her sleeveless white blouse. "You look like a college kid."

She laughed breathlessly, making a lie of her words, "College, yes. Kid, no." Lord, but he made her feel like a kid. A giddy kid. Whatever was happening here, she knew she liked it, couldn't fight it, maybe even shouldn't fight it. But . . . what if it wasn't happening for him the same way it was for her? There was so much danger in being this madly attracted to a man who called himself Stud.

She gave his clothing the once-over again, laughter fading. "Off to work?" She knew he'd been working at his new job for most of the week, but this was the first time she'd seen him dressed for it. He looked quite . . . respectable. She wished she didn't feel so happy about that.

He tugged at his tie. "To work, but first to see the bank manager."

"You're going to ride your bike dressed in a suit and tie?"

"No," he said, sliding one hand under her stack of books, lifting them away from her and setting them on the trunk of a blue sedan parked nearby. "My new car." He patted the shining finish of the car near where he'd dumped her books. "Didn't you notice it was parked in your slot?"

She shook her head. "I was hardly aware that that was my slot."

He looked quizzical. "Why don't you have a car?"

Mary hesitated, then shrugged. "I don't need one. There's always a bus or a taxi or the Skytrain where I want to go."

"Can you drive?"

She looked down. For a moment the past twisted around her, and she stared into its narrow gorge, watching horror turn and swirl like black water. "Yes," she said, her voice low. "I can drive. I choose not to."

He tilted her face up, looked at her searchingly,

but whatever shadows might have been there for a moment were gone now. She smiled. "You should be grateful. If Mr. Taylor gave you this slot, you won't have to park one of your vehicles on the street. Most of the people here with two cars do."

"He gave it to me because you and I are friends, so, of course, I'm grateful," he said, bending a little closer. "Why don't I show you how grateful?" His thumb stroked her lips, making her shiver with pleasure she was sure he must be able to feel through his skin.

Their eyes met. They were both remembering that kiss the other evening. "Why don't we just accept that I believe you're grateful?" she said.

"You're no fun at all," he complained. "But I do thank you. This way I can have a car for work and my bike for play, and park them both off the street." He grinned down at her and tapped her nose with one finger. "Will you come out and play with this lily of the field for a while tomorrow?"

She shook her head. "I'll be toiling—studying—and you'll need to sleep."

As if the mention of sleep triggered it, he yawned widely, patting his mouth with the back of his hand. "I'll get some sleep, you do some reading, and then we can play for a while. I promise to be quiet when I come in from work," he added, as if by behaving himself he might earn a reward.

Mary suppressed a smile. "I doubt that you'll bother me unless you go out on your balcony and sing. After all, you live on the second floor. I live on the third."

"You make that sound like East is East and West is West," he said. "I've missed you these past few days, Mary, but I left you alone to work." He grinned, wrinkling his nose. "Playing all by myself isn't much fun."

Really, the man seemed obsessed with fun! Of course, he'd just had two days off; he'd said that he didn't work on Sundays and Mondays. "Didn't you get any sleep today?" she asked. "The first night shift of each week is always the hardest. You should try to rest before you go to work."

His laughter held a teasing note. "Yes, Mother."

"Oh. Sorry." She felt a flush rising up in her face and looked down, reaching for her books. "Not my business."

He chuckled softly, hands on her waist, turning her so she couldn't pick up her homework. "It's okay, Mary. I like it when you say things that show you care about my well-being." His warm fingers touched her under the chin, tilting her face up. "Do you care about me enough to give me an off-to-work kiss?"

His green-hazel eyes were dancing and filled with a warmth that she felt right into her bones. No wonder that poor teacher, Evelyn, had succumbed to the Hagendorn charm even without promises of forever. She tried to pull away from him, but his left hand was flat on the small of her back, his right still under her chin, caressing her throat. She wondered if he could feel the wild pulse there. "I couldn't do that. You might be late for work." Her voice was unexpectedly husky.

His grin was full of mischief. "What kind of kiss are you thinking about? A quick off-to-work kiss wouldn't make me late. But if you have something else in mind, I'm willing to go for it. Jake can't fire me. I'm his partner."

"I . . . Well, uh, oh!" She was embarrassed and didn't quite know why. Of course a quick little kiss wouldn't make him late for work. She thought about stepping away, but something held her there, frozen. The mesmerizing thought of even a brief kiss shared with him kept her enthralled.

He chuckled at her discomfort, and she saw for the first time that he had a dimple beside the left-hand corner of his mouth, partially concealed by the downward angle of his mustache. She wanted very, very badly to place her lips over it. "Just a little kiss," he said softly, leaning ever closer. She could feel his breath on her cheek.

"All right, just a little one," she said, hearing alarm bells clanging loudly in her head and seeing growing hunger in his eyes, hunger that she knew must be echoed in her own, because it filled her blood with a rampant need she could no longer deny.

"We'll have to settle for that, I guess," he said, drawing her closer. Their bodies touched along the length of them, knee to knee, thigh to thigh, belly to belly, chest to breast. He took his hand from under her chin and placed it on her back, beside the other. She didn't lower her face. "This time," he added quietly, and she felt his breath on her lips, but no kiss, not yet.

"This time . . . what?"

"A little kiss this time. But next time . . ." His lips were just brushing hers as his voice trailed off. She placed her hands on his chest, fingers curling against the lapels of his dark blue suit, not clinging but not shoving him back either. The fabric of his suit was smooth and yet very masculine, as masculine as the scent that arose from his body, surrounding her, filling her.

"Bruce . . ." Was that funny little thread of sound her voice? Her lips were too dry. She moistened them with the tip of her tongue.

"I think," he said softly, "that I could learn to like my name after all. If you were to say it that way all the time."

"Bruce . . ."

"Yes. Just . . . like . . . that," he murmured, taking little nips of her lips before he lifted his head again, as if to assess her reaction. She touched her bottom lip with the tip of her tongue in a vain attempt at stilling its tingling.

"Again," he murmured, and she didn't know if he

meant he was going to kiss her like that again, or if he wanted her to say his name again, or moisten her lip . . .

"Bruce . . ." she whispered, and saw him smile, then saw nothing as her eyes fluttered closed and his mouth covered hers with a hard, insistent warmth. This was not turning out to be a little kiss, a quick kiss, a friendly off-to-work kiss. This was turning out to be something a whole lot more. And in her mind a small voice said it one more time. . . . *Oh . . . Bruce!*

He took her lips with his, parted them with no trouble at all, and plunged his tongue deep inside as he drew her more tightly against his body. Without thought she succumbed dizzily to his sensual touch. His mustache was soft, silky, brushing just under her nose, at the corners of her mouth. His lips were firm and hot, and his tongue captured hers, toyed with it, drew it out and into his mouth where he sucked on it gently then let it go. She copied his actions, tempting his to follow hers, flicking the inside of his lower lip with the tip of her tongue, then nibbling gently with her teeth.

He shifted his hold on her and made it easy for her to slide her arms up around his neck. He nuzzled her throat, tugged on her earlobe, flattened his palms down along her sides, then curved them over her hips, dragging her even more tightly against the rising hardness she felt at his front. He murmured her name against her throat, returned to her mouth for endless moments, then slid his lips over her cheeks, her eyelids, her neck.

She could have cried with the beauty of the feelings growing and exploding inside her, could have sung with joy at recovering something she'd long thought lost to her, but she was too busy enjoying herself to do either. She tangled her hands in his hair, angled her face, and moved his head so that his lips were back over hers as they drank deeply of each other. Oh, Lord, how she wanted this! How she needed it! Needed him. His scent filled her nostrils. His taste filled her mouth. His bulk filled her arms. His hair tickled her palms and fingers and the sound of his rasping breath thrilled her. Her heart hammered hard, her nipples engorged, nearly burst through her clothing as she moved against him, moaning softly.

A horn honked. Another one. A car door slammed close by, and someone gave a shrill wolf whistle. Somebody applauded, and someone else shouted something that sounded vaguely like "Way to go!" Mary heard, but only on one level, and it was on a level so far down as to be easily ignored.

Not so Bruce. Slowly, bemusedly, he lifted his head, looking down at her, frowning slightly as if he weren't sure who she was, maybe not even sure who *he* was, and for the first time in many moments, Mary became horrifyingly aware of *where* she was.

"Oh, my God!" she said, snatching her arms from around his neck, tearing herself out of his tight embrace. "What's going on here? What am I doing?"

"Good question," he said, steadying her as she tried to spin away from him only to bash into the trunk of his car, half-blind with passion and embarrassment and unfulfilled need. He held her upright against him, looking deeply into her darkened, confused blue eyes.

She could see a pulse hammering rapidly in his temple, feel him trembling as she trembled, hear the breathlessness of his tone, see the agitated rise and fall of his chest. Okay, she thought dimly, so it hadn't just happened to her, whatever it was that had happened. It had happened to both of them. The combination of them. Volatile. Potent. Exciting.

"That's a great question," he said. "What are you doing, Mary DeLaney? To me?"

What was she doing to him? She couldn't think, couldn't reply, so busy was her brain trying to sort out what had happened to *her*. Where had it come from, that wild, irrepressible need, that instantaneous combustion between the two of them? Was it the result of a combination of his expertise and her hunger? She looked at him, saw that he was as confused as she was, and that the desire eating away at her was even yet attacking him just as strongly. That long embrace, those heated kisses had done nothing to diminish it. In either of them.

"I'm going inside," she said, wrenching herself free again, gathering up her books and holding them in front of her like a shield. She couldn't look at him; she certainly couldn't look at the neighbors who were coming home from work, parking their cars, glancing over at her and Bruce. Which ones had honked? Who had whistled? How many had recognized her? So much for the anonymity of a big city! Do something dumb, and everyone you know gets to watch! Especially if you do it in your own front yard.

"Going in?" he said, clamping her shoulders in his trembling hands. "Right now? No! You can't walk away from it, Mary! From me. From this."

"Bruce . . . let me go. You'll be late for your appointment."

He was damned if he'd let her go, leaving him all steamed and tight like this. He didn't give a hoot about being late at the bank. His partner would understand. Hell, he thought, it'd be a good thing if someone understood. He sure as hell didn't. Not completely, anyway. But he sure had his suspicions! If this wasn't love, then it was so much like everything he'd ever heard about love that it had to be a damned close approximation. Close enough for him. But was it the same for her? That was the important question.

"We have to talk about what happened, Mary. It's important. To both of us. What happened here isn't something we can turn our backs on. We have to

. . . deal with it. Isn't that what you psychologists always say? Deal with things? Face them? Okay then, deal with this. Face it. And help me do the same."

"Yes. I mean, no. There is nothing to deal with, I mean. You kissed me. That's all."

"Ahh, Mary! You're such a liar. That was more than me kissing you. You kissed, too, you know. You kissed me like you'd been aching to kiss me for forty years. We have to deal with that, with what we just did to each other. I can't handle this all alone. We've started something here. What are we going to do about it?"

"Nothing. Nothing at all." Tears sprang to her eyes, choked her voice. "Good-bye. Good night. And if you kiss all the ladies you escort like that, your business is sure to be a roaring success."

She wheeled away and made for the door, hoping her legs would hold her up until she was safely inside her own apartment. She never looked back to see Bruce Hagendorn standing there staring after her as if she were completely out of her mind. Or as if he were out of his.

He shook his head, got into his car, tried to put it in gear, then remembered he had to put the key in the ignition and start the engine first. *Ladies? Escort?* What in the world had she been talking about?

And did it really matter? He smiled, shaking his head, forcing himself to regain a whole lot more control before backing out of his parking slot. He'd be a menace on the streets like this. For several moments more he sat there, thinking. Sometimes what people said wasn't important at all. It was what they did that counted. And Mary DeLaney had just done something to him that had never been done before. He was determined that she was going to do it again.

And again. And again.

• • •

"Aggie, are you busy tonight?"

"Never too busy for you. What's up?"

"Nothing, really. I just don't feel like studying. I wondered if we could maybe get together."

"Hey, great. I'd love that. Steve's out of town so why don't you come on over? We'll have dinner after I put Mark to bed, and then watch a video or two if you like, or just sit and talk. Okay?"

"Wonderful!" Mary didn't try to disguise the relief in her voice. No way could she have spent the evening alone. She'd have driven herself nuts rehashing what had happened. She was overwhelmed with needless, futile, stupid guilt and just as many needless, futile, and stupid questions, to say nothing of the burning, aching need for more of what Bruce Hagendorn had given her. "I'll be there in half an hour."

"Well, well, well," said Aggie, giving her a sweeping look as she opened the door, grinning as she looked at her friend with eyes that Mary knew saw more than she wanted her to see. But there was no hiding it. "A man! Who is he?" She hitched her wet, naked son onto her other hip and turned through the door. "Come on out to the patio and tell me everything."

"There's nothing to tell," said Mary, sinking down in the deck chair her friend swung around for her. She watched Mark splash back into his wading pool and felt a hot blush climbing from the top of her sundress up her chest and neck to her face, thinking about someone else in a wading pool. He hadn't been naked like the child was, but . . .

"You don't say." Aggie gave her a look of pure mischief. "You blush like that and tell me there's nothing to tell?"

"Well, not a lot."

"Ah-ha! Now we're getting somewhere. You sit tight

and watch my son for me. I'll get the wine. That'll get things going."

"No thanks, Aggie, none for me," Mary said, but her friend was gone, moving lightly and quickly as she always did. Like a butterfly, Mary always thought, or a hummingbird. Maybe a dragonfly.

"This," said Aggie, "can be considered medicinal."

"No, thanks." Mary shook her head resolutely. "But you go ahead."

"Yeah. I thought you'd say that. So I brought you some soda." Aggie lifted a tall, steamy glass from a table behind Mary and put it in her hand before sitting down nearby with the wineglass. "Okay, what happened?" She took a tiny sip, eyeing her friend expectantly over the rim.

"I met a man. He lives in my building. He gave me a lift to class one afternoon, we had dinner that evening before I went to work, he picked me up the following morning, and . . . well, I've seen him a time or two."

"And?"

"And this afternoon he kissed me."

"Oh. . . . That serious, huh? When's the wedding?"

"Ag—" Mary took a large gulp of her drink and set it down again. "Don't make fun of me, okay?"

Aggie patted her arm. "Hey, somebody has to. You're being a dope. So the guy kissed you. I assume you kissed him back?"

Mary had to smile as she remembered. "Oh, yes. You could say that." Suddenly she laughed aloud. "Boy, did I kiss him back!"

"Fireworks?"

"Chinese New Year, the closing night of Expo, and Halloween all rolled into one."

"And now you're feeling all cut up inside, riddled with guilt."

"Something like that." Mary bit her lip. "But I'm trying not to. Honest, Aggie. I just can't help it, I guess. I keep thinking about Kevin." But what made it worse, she knew, was that she was thinking about Bruce a lot more than she was about her late husband.

"Kid, you've been a widow for over four years," Aggie said kindly, and Mary knew she really did understand. Aggie always did. That was why she'd come. "Kevin wouldn't have wanted you to do this to yourself. So quit doing it. Go back to your guy. Kiss him again. And enjoy."

"I . . . did enjoy. But so do countless others, I gather. Have you ever heard of Stud Hagendorn?"

"Holy cow!" Aggie's eyes widened into huge brown orbs. "Who hasn't?"

"Me. I mean, I hadn't. Until a week ago last Friday. Or if I had, I never paid any attention to the name."

"You mean . . . ?"

Mary nodded. "And he's a partner in an escort service."

"So?" Aggie was startled, Mary knew, but she tried to be nonchalant. "Somebody has to run escort services, I suppose," she added lamely, a frown forming between her brows.

"Assuming they're necessary in the first place, I guess you're right. What I don't know about Bruce is if he's a partner who just works in the office and arranges . . . uh . . . dates for other people, or if he goes out and . . ."

"Escorts?" Aggie asked dryly, always the one to get right to the gist of the matter. She was frowning more deeply.

"Right. There are guys who do that, you know. And women who . . . pay them."

"I do know. But I thought we were talking about a hockey player. Did I miss something somewhere? Who is this Bruce?"

"Bruce Hagendorn. Stud is his nickname. For obvious reasons, I'm told, though not by him. And he's not a hockey player any longer. He's retired."

"Oh! Yes, I knew that, of course. I guess I'd forgotten," Aggie said, sipping her wine. "Now, suppose you tell me what the real problem is."

"What do you mean? I just did! I'm half-sick with guilt I know I should't feel but feel anyway, and the man I'm interested in might have the morals of an alley cat. That's the problem, Aggie, and I don't know what to do about it."

"Okay, okay, cool down." Aggie got to her feet and scooped up her wet, shivering son, wrapping him in a towel in spite of his protests.

"Let's get this little guy into bed, then we can eat and talk properly," she said. "You can make the salad to go with the tuna casserole while I take care of Mark. Okay?"

Mary nodded, getting to her feet. "And don't worry," said her friend. "We'll get it all sorted out. Cheer up."

After dinner, curled in a big chair in the den, Aggie sipped her coffee and looked at Mary over the rim of her cup. "Okay. I've had some time to think. I admit guilt could play a big part in your ambivalence about this new relationship, at least at first, but you're too sensible to let that bother you for long. And your concerns about Stud Hagendorn's morals might be valid, but if it were just that, you'd simply walk away. So what gives?"

"I . . . think maybe I'm in danger of falling in love with him. And I'm scared, Ag. Awfully scared. We're really very different."

"Hey, there's nothing wrong with falling in love with a man who's a bit different from you. Remember the old adage, opposites attract. Falling in love is wonderful. Nothing scary about it at all. Give in to it, Mare. Let it happen. You know, go with the flow."

"Aggie, it's not that easy."

"Why not? You're obviously halfway in love with the guy already. It seems he must like you, or he wouldn't have taken you out, to say nothing of picking you up after work. Most people avoid the slums. So I don't see a problem."

"Well, I do! How can I be halfway in love with a guy who runs an escort service, for heaven's sake? I mean, it's not exactly what I'd call a respectable profession!"

"Oh, come on! You're not being snobbish about this, are you, without even knowing what kind of escort service he's involved with? I know Kevin was a professional man with great prospects, but . . ." Aggie shrugged.

"No!" said Mary in angry protest. "No, it's not like that at all! I wouldn't care if Bruce dug ditches or climbed telephone poles to string wire or slung hash in a low-class diner or was a brain surgeon or a wealthy financier. What any person does for a living is unimportant to me as long as the living they earn is honest. You know me better than that. But there's something . . . I don't know . . . unsavory, I guess, about the escort-for-hire business in most people's minds. It reeks of . . ."

"Pimping?"

"Yes," Mary said unhappily.

"Okay, I can see where you're coming from." Aggie lifted her coffee again, sipping at it thoughtfully for a few minutes. "What did your Stud say when you asked him about what kind of escort service he works for? Did it sound like one of the good ones, or one of the shady ones?"

"Oh, I haven't discussed it with him. He's never even mentioned it to me. I found out about his work indirectly. In fact, he won't talk about it at all. Every time I ask about his job, he gets . . . evasive, as if he's ashamed of it. So I suspect it probably isn't one of the good kind of escort services. I told myself that it didn't matter what he did, that he had every right to his privacy, because we were nothing more than casual friends, acquaintances really, but then today things changed. Sort of."

"For you alone? Or for both of you?"

"I don't know." Mary pushed her cuticles back

with a thumbnail. "At the time he seemed just as affected by what happened as I was. He wanted to discuss it right there and then in the parking lot with everyone watching and maybe listening."

Aggie grinned. "The parking lot? Where?"

"In front of our building."

Aggie laughed. "You were necking in a car? Good for you! It's about time you started acting like real folks again. Remember when you and Kevin and Steve and I went—"

"Not in a car," Mary said miserably, hardly hearing her friend's last sentence. "In the parking lot." She lifted her head and gazed at Aggie. "In broad daylight. In full view of everyone coming home from work. People honked their horns. One guy whistled. A couple of people applauded." She frowned bemusedly. "And you know what? I heard all that, recognized what I was hearing, knew what we were doing was the cause of it, and still didn't want to stop. Bruce was the one who stopped."

Aggie's smile gentled. "That's all right, Mary. There's no law against getting carried away by a kiss. And I still think it's about time."

"That's part of what worries me. What if I only responded to him like that because he's the first man I've really kissed since Kevin died? Would I respond like that to anybody? Am I just a sex-starved woman who's pushing thirty and willing to reach out and grab any guy who walks by too close?"

Aggie thought for a moment or two, looking at Mary, her head tilted to one side. Then, with a shrug, she said, "I don't know. Why don't you get yourself into the position of finding out? Why not date someone else, encourage him to kiss you and see what happens? See if the fireworks are purely Stud Hagendorn generated."

Mary thought about that, then shuddered. "Not a good idea. Even thinking about kissing any of the men who've been asking me out the past four years makes me feel uncomfortable."

"I see. And what does thinking about kissing your Stud make you feel?"

Mary sighed and ran her hands into her hair, shoving it back behind her ears. "I think you know."

"And I think that's your answer, friend."

"Yes," Mary agreed. "I guess maybe it is." She got to her feet. "Thanks, Ag. I knew it would help to talk things over with you."

Aggie rose, too, and slipped an arm through Mary's as they walked to the door. "Bring him to meet us one day soon. Steve will go ape when I tell him about your Stud."

Mary laughed. "Dammit, I wish you'd quit referring to the man as my stud. He's not!"

Aggie gave her a hug. "Isn't he?" But Mary didn't answer. She just looked at her friend, her eyes and heart and mind full of questions, then turned and jogged all the way to the Skytrain station three long uphill blocks away.

As she walked the last couple of blocks home, she shivered with delicious anticipation at the prospect of seeing Bruce and finding even more answers to her mind full of agitated questions. But the primary one was: When will I see him again?

Stud fell asleep at four in the morning still wondering about Mary's strange statement about the women he escorted, and woke up with the sound of her voice in his ears. He hugged his pillow, knowing he'd been dreaming of her, and squeezed his eyes shut against the gray light of the room.

Gray? Not golden? Every morning since he'd arrived in Vancouver had been golden and warm and welcoming. He listened to a steady hissing sound, a wet sibilance that seemed to chill the air.

He opened his eyes again. It was raining. A cool, damp breeze blew in his open window, salt scented. He sat up. Well. He knew it rained on the coast, but this was the first rainy day since he'd come. He wasn't going to waste it. If he was going to phone home and talk about the weather out here, then he'd better learn about all of its aspects. Besides, people back in Manitoba would expect him to have lots of rainy-day stories about the coast, expect him to have grown webbed feet already. So far no one was happy believing that he'd lived there for over two weeks and hadn't seen a drop of wet stuff falling from the skies.

"Bruce!" He cocked his head and listened. "Bruce!" Mary! That *was* her voice. He hadn't been dreaming. He loped out of his bedroom and across the living room, slid open the door to the patio, and came to a screeching halt. He was buck naked.

Snatching up a pillow, he held it in front of him and stepped outside, looking up. She was leaning on the rail facing his apartment, her hair plastered to her head. The wind was whipping the lace of a frothy little garment against her neck, and the rain was sticking it to her beautiful breasts, turning it transparent. The rest of her nightgown was soaked and sticking to her and completely see-through too. His mouth opened and closed several times before he could manage to speak.

"What's wrong?"

"Hi," she said. "Sorry to wake you up. But I need help."

"What's wrong?" he repeated. Brother! He was croaking like an old crow, and his vocabulary seemed to have deserted him. All he could do was stare like a sex-obsessed twelve-year-old! He'd seen wet women before, for pete's sake! But how many wet women, a little voice inside asked, had he seen who looked exactly like Mary DeLaney did wet?

"I'm stuck out here. The door's jammed. And I'm freezing to death. Would you please call Mr. Taylor and ask him to come up?"

"I . . ." He swallowed. "Sure. One minute. Hang

on. Don't leave." He frowned. What was he saying? Of course she wouldn't leave. She was stuck. And wet. And freezing to death. And wet. He could have spent the rest of the day staring up at her, but he clamped his jaw shut and turned to go inside. He heard her giggle and realized that the cushion he held hid only his front. He stared at her over his shoulder for a moment, then slid through the open door, wondering why he felt so abashed at having her see him bare-assed in the rain. He bit his lip and glanced down and around, wondering if she'd liked what she saw. Was his flesh still as tight and as firm as he hoped? Had he presented a pleasing picture to her? He had never worried about a thing like that before. He grimaced, strode into his bedroom, and turned, craning his neck over his shoulder, trying for a better view in the mirror. Damn the woman! What was she doing to him, anyway?

He groaned. What was she doing? She was standing out in the rain wearing a Stretch 'n Seal nightgown, waiting for him to come and save her. His heart lurched inside his chest, and he whirled, tugging on a tracksuit, all the while thinking of how grateful she'd be to him for rescuing her. She'd fling herself into his arms—her wet, cold self. She'd cling to him for warmth, and he'd hold her shivering body in his arms. Her wet, shivering body clad only in that thin wisp of nylon that hid nothing and . . . and he'd kiss her the way he had the day before, only this time there wouldn't be anyone to honk or whistle or stop them. And he'd peel her out of that wet garment so she wouldn't catch pneumonia and . . .

Stud groaned again and bolted out the door.

six

"I'd like to buy an *E*, please."

Stud's knock on the super's door failed to override the sound of the television.

"That's a fine buy, Caroline. There are, let's count them . . . one, two, three, *four* of them. That should help you out."

Stud knocked louder, and rang the bell just as a surge of applause arose as Caroline solved the puzzle. A commercial extolling the virtues of a sinus medicine came on while he was ringing for the second time, and then he heard the grumbling voice of the super. "Just a minute! Hold your horses." The door jerked open. "What—well, Stud, boy. Come on in."

"Listen, Jerry, just give me a key to Mary DeLaney's apartment, okay?" he said urgently.

"Hah! That's some kind of joke, right?" Taylor snorted in appreciation. "Come on in, boy. I'll make you some coffee."

"No, not now, Jerry. I don't want to interrupt your television show. Just let me have that key, please!"

"Now, now." Taylor gave Stud a chiding look. "Don't want to knock a guy for living up to his name, but that little gal isn't for the likes of you. She never dates, never goes out. You stick with the ones who can handle what you've got," he added with a grin, returning his attention to the TV screen, which was visible through the doorway.

The commercial was over and someone named Ariel was spinning the wheel, her long hair draping down. Stud thought of Mary's wet hair dripping down over her shoulders, wetting the front of her nightgown. . . .

"Jerry," he croaked, "I need to go help her. Her balcony door is stuck."

"Oh. Is that all? Those doors stick all the time. Just needs a shot of oil. I'll take care of it. In a minute or two," the super added, turning back to his television, taking a couple of sidling steps closer to it.

"Thirty-five hundred dollars, Ariel. Give us a letter, please."

"Jerry, she's stuck out there on her balcony."

"Yeah, yeah. I understand that. I'll go up in a minute."

"Is there an *N*?"

"There is indeed." The little chime rang three times as Vanna turned the letters, and Stud spoke into a roar of cheers and applause from an unseen audience.

"She's stuck out there in the rain!"

His words went unheard while the woman named Ariel looked stunned and scared and delighted, then spun again as Jerry Taylor stared, mesmerized, at the blur of the wheel.

Snatching the spare key to apartment number 317, Stud turned and ran out, shaking his head. He bolted up the stairs, entered Mary's apartment, and checked out the patio door that was causing the problem. He placed the flat of his hand on the rain-streaked glass, giving it a shake, seeing Mary, blurred, huddled as close to the wall as she could get. The door would not budge. He flipped the lock mechanism several times, then began systematically pounding all around the perimeter of the frame, hoping to dislodge whatever might be jamming it.

OPEN YOUR HEART TO LOVE...
YOU'LL BE LOVESWEPT WITH THIS FREE OFFER!

HERE'S WHAT YOU GET:

1. **FREE!** SIX NEW LOVESWEPT NOVELS! You get 6 beautiful stories filled with passion, romance, laughter, and tears... exciting romances to stir the excitement of falling in love... again and again.

2. **FREE!** A BEAUTIFUL MAKEUP CASE WITH A MIRROR THAT LIGHTS UP! What could be more useful than a makeup case with a mirror that lights up*? Once you open the tortoise-shell finish case, you have a choice of brushes... for your lips, your eyes, and your blushing cheeks.

*(batteries not included)

3. **SAVE!** MONEY-SAVING HOME DELIVERY! Join the Loveswept at-home reader service and we'll send you 6 new novels each month. You always get 15 days to preview them before you decide. Each book is yours for only $2.09 — a savings of 41¢ per book.

4. **BEAT THE CROWDS!** You'll always receive your Loveswept books before they are available in bookstores. You'll be the first to thrill to these exciting new stories.

BE LOVESWEPT TODAY — JUST COMPLETE, DETACH AND MAIL YOUR FREE-OFFER CARD.

GET READY TO BE LOVESWEPT!

YES! Please send my six Loveswept novels FREE, along with my free lighted makeup case as explained on the opposite page.

Loveswept

PLACE
HEART
STICKER
HERE

NAME _____

ADDRESS _____ APT. ____

CITY _____

STATE _____ ZIP _____

10355

MY "NO RISK" GUARANTEE:

There's no obligation to buy — the free gifts are mine to keep. I may preview each subsequent shipment for 15 days. If I don't want it, I simply return the books within 15 days and owe nothing. If I keep them I will pay just $12.50 (I save $2.50 off the retail price for 6 books) plus postage and handling and any applicable sales tax.

Prices subject to change. Orders subject to approval.

BRo

• NO PURCHASE NECESSARY
• NO OBLIGATION
FREE – 6 LOVESWEPT NOVELS!
FREE – LIGHTED MAKEUP CASE!

(DETACH AND MAIL CARD TODAY.)

NO POSTAGE
NECESSARY
IF MAILED
IN THE
UNITED STATES

BUSINESS REPLY MAIL
FIRST-CLASS MAIL   PERMIT NO. 2456   HICKSVILLE, N.Y.

POSTAGE WILL BE PAID BY ADDRESSEE

Loveswept

Bantam Books
P.O. Box 985
Hicksville, NY 11802-9827

REMEMBER!

- The free books and gift are mine to keep!
- There is no obligation!
- I may preview each shipment for 15 days!
- I can cancel anytime!

He hammered the door several times before it gave up the fight and slid open several inches, just enough for her to slip inside. She shoved her wet hair off her face and stared at him. He waited for her to run to him, to cling to him, to fling her arms around his waist, but her blue eyes blazed with indignation instead of gratitude.

"What are you doing here?" she demanded. "I asked you to send Mr. Taylor." Damn! She hated having him see her with her hair all flat and wet and dripping! She didn't have on a lick of makeup and must look like a scarecrow!

"The . . . uh . . . *Wheel of Fortune* . . ." he said lamely, his eyes traveling from the top of her wet head to the tips of her pink-painted toenails, missing no detail in between. Dainty lace outlined rounded breasts with rosy, puckered, pointed tips. A neatly indented waist flared out into curvaceous hips and a tidy little belly button made a dimple in the transparent fabric. Her thighs were everything he'd dreamed of since first seeing them sprawled on his couch, and again he was caught up in the desire to run his hands up them, part them, move between them. He licked his lips as his eyes made the return trip even more slowly, and his hands clenched at his sides. He tried to say something, but only a soft groan came from his throat, more like a growl of pure male lust.

Mary looked down at herself, eyes widening as she saw exactly what he was seeing. This was a thousand times worse than having him see her looking like a scarecrow! This was . . . She gave an outraged gasp, then wheeled and ran for the bathroom even as he lifted one hand to stop her. It just brushed down her back as she spun away from him, and he was left holding nothing but air.

"Mary! Wait!"

"Out!" she said over her shoulder. "You get out of here right now, Bruce Hagendorn! You . . . you voyeur, you!"

Mary slammed the bathroom door behind her, locked it, and stood staring at herself in the mirror. Her nightgown was completely transparent. Her nipples jutted out like little sentinels, and she knew that the effect had little to do with being cold. She was reacting, reacting wildly to the look in Bruce Hagendorn's eyes, the open craving on his face. He had looked at her and wanted her.

She shivered and turned on the shower, stepping under the hot spray and slithering out of her wet garment. And she had looked right back.

And wanted him. It took a long time for her breathing to return to normal.

He stood there, still seeing in his mind's eye the sight she had made, then slowly backed up until he came to a chair. He sat down and waited for her to come out. Inside his head the picture of her body spun around and around and around. And inside his heart something he had never felt before grew larger and heavier and more momentous by the second until he could hardly breathe around it.

He listened to the sound of her shower, pictured the warm water streaming over her, dripping from her hair, beading on her shoulders, crystal drops forming on her nipples. His tongue came out as if he could lick them off, and his body hardened as he fantasized about her. When the shower stopped, he visualized her drying herself with a big, soft towel. He groaned softly again, helplessly, and knew he should leave before she emerged. She had told him to go. She hadn't been happy he'd rescued her. She hadn't flung herself gratefully into his arms. She hadn't tilted her face up for a kiss as she had the afternoon before. She had seen him ogling her, been heartily offended, and had run from him. He was just as heartily disgusted with himself, but he still couldn't manage to leave.

He listened to the sound of a blow dryer for several minutes, heard it shut off, and sat watching as she opened the door—cautiously, he noticed—glanced around and spotted him. Quickly she shut it again. "I told you to go!" Her voice was only slightly muffled by the door.

He stood, walked to the bathroom door, and leaned on the wall. "I'm not leaving," he said quietly, stubbornly.

"Well, you certainly can't stay!" She sounded mostly embarrassed, not really mad, he thought. She opened the door again and came out, a frown on her broad brow, her hair a soft, curly tumble on her shoulders, her slender body fully hidden by that damned blue bathrobe. He wondered giddily what she had on under it, and felt himself harden again. Impatiently he shouldered his body away from the wall and strode back into the living room, sensing her following him.

"I can stay long enough for you to explain what you meant by that crack yesterday," he said, turning to face her.

Mary tilted her head to one side, tugged the sash of her robe a little tighter, and said, "What crack?"

"The one about the ladies I'm supposed to be escorting, and how if I kiss them the way I kissed you, my business would soon be booming."

"Well, let's face it, Bruce, when you kiss a woman, she knows she's been kissed. You are an expert. You kiss better than anyone I've ever kissed. No wonder you're called Stud! It makes me wonder what would happen to me if you made love to me, considering what you can do to me with just a kiss and . . . Oh!" She whirled away from him, turning her back. "What am I saying? Dammit, what is it you do to me that makes me run off at the mouth and say the dumbest things in the world? I've never talked to another man the way I talk to you and—"

He stepped closer and caught her shoulders, set her down into a chair, and stood over her. "Well?"

"Well, what?" Her face was flaming. She refused to meet his eyes.

"What ladies?"

"The . . . the ones at the escort service."

He shook his head in confusion and sat down across from her on the sofa. "What escort service might that be?"

"Your escort service." He opened his mouth to speak, but she waved a hand, cutting him off. "Oh, I realize that you didn't want me to know about it, that that's why you were being so vague about your job. I wondered if even your partner's wife knows what kind of business he runs, even though that seems pretty strange in this day and age, and I realize why you didn't want Evelyn involved with it, or even aware of it, but I'm not a wife or a girlfriend, so you can go ahead and confide in me. You see, Bruce, I saw what you had circled in the paper. Escort services. Three of them. One right after another. And what other kind of business has the kind of hours you keep?"

She continued to look at him when he failed to respond. "Do you know that your mouth is open?" she asked kindly.

With great difficulty he closed it. Then he opened it again, threw back his head, and laughed.

"What's so darned funny?" Mary demanded, getting to her feet, angry and embarrassed all over again.

"You are," said Bruce. "Escort service! Me?"

"Yes, you." She was annoyed at him for laughing at her. "I know what I saw, Bruce. Three ads in your paper, circled with big black rings. It was right there on your coffee table in plain view that day I came in to help you after I threw the flowers at you."

"That may be true, but have you ever circled things in the paper with a marker? It soaks right through, remember? I don't know what I'd marked on the other side of that sheet of newspaper, but I sure wasn't thinking about joining any escort service."

She bit her lip, recognizing the truth of his words. Marker ink did soak through. Why hadn't she thought of that? And why, oh why, hadn't she kept her big mouth shut? "Oh. I see. I'm sorry."

He laughed again. "I love it! You thought I was out there selling my body to lonely ladies? You really thought that of me?" He broke off as she turned away from him, but not so quickly that he didn't see a glimpse of her chagrined, flushed face.

"Well, if not your body, then at least your companionship. I know there are different kinds of escort services. Sort of."

"Ah, Mary." Gently he turned her and tilted her face up to his. "Look at me."

Reluctantly she did so.

"Why did it matter to you so much, thinking I did something like that?"

"Because I want . . . wanted to be able to respect you and . . ." She let her sentence trail off, grimacing in self-disgust. "Of course, it's none of my business what you do with your life."

"Sure it is," he said quietly. "Haven't we agreed to be friends?" His fingers gripped her shoulders more tightly. His face looked momentarily vulnerable. "And I think we're going to become more than that, aren't we?"

"More?"

"Much more. I've been thinking about that a lot since yesterday in the parking lot. Haven't you?"

She nodded.

"We're going to be lovers, Mary," he said, drawing her firmly against his body. "Lovers, at the very least."

She swallowed hard, feeling dizzy and scared and excited, totally aware that she was wearing nothing but her bathrobe and that he must know it too.

"Right now?" she asked, and could have kicked herself for the quavering squeak of her voice and for the stupid question. Right now, indeed, as if she didn't have any say in the matter at all. And she did. Of course she did. Trouble was, she didn't have the faintest idea what she might say if she dared to open her mouth again.

Bruce laughed at her, but it was a soft laugh, one full of affection and tenderness and happiness as he stroked a soft touch down the side of her cheek to her throat. "Don't I wish!" he said, smiling that smile of his that warmed her right through to the middle. "But no, Mary, not right now. Soon. When we know each other a little better. We need to be good friends first. There's no need to look so alarmed."

"Was I?"

"You were." He bent his head to give her a small, reassuring kiss.

"If you say so," she said, smiling up at him. Then, "So if you haven't joined up with an escort service, what does your partnership entail?"

His eyes were half-closed, and for just an instant, they popped wide, looking almost frightened, but then he was nuzzling at her mouth again. "Kissing pretty brunettes in blue bathrobes."

"Really?" It was hard to speak. "What an interesting way to make a living. And your partner does it too?"

"Not if I catch him at it," he said, his lips moving gently over her cheek, down her neck. "At least not if I catch him kissing this pretty brunette in this blue bathrobe."

"Not a chance of that happening," she murmured, liking the raspy feel of his skin against hers, the silk of his mustache as it brushed over her lip. "I don't know the guy, and I never kiss men I don't know."

"Then you think you know me well enough?"

"Mmm, for a kiss . . . or two. . . ."

"Or three?"

"Mmm. . . ."

She turned her face, and at the touch of her soft lips, he moaned, dragging her tightly against him, tasting her, exploring, feeding their mutual need until he thought he would explode and she would melt in his arms. Slowly he lifted his head, looking down at her pink face, her closed lids, her long lashes. Slowly those lashes fluttered up, and she gazed into his eyes, bemused.

He wanted her! Lord, how he wanted her! How had he lived for thirty-six years without ever feeling anything even remotely close to what he felt now? He knew he should step back, that the time wasn't right, that they hadn't known each other long enough, that the one big issue between them remained unresolved. But he needed just one more taste of her. He closed his eyes, dipped his head again, and found her lips, feeling her blissful sigh against his skin.

Her lips parted for him, and she gave him her soul as her body moved against him in a rhythm that matched the thrusting of his tongue against hers. It was a deep and heady meeting, and he couldn't think, didn't want to, wanted only to lose himself in the scent of her skin, the silk of her hair, the texture of it in his hands. He ached to strip that robe off her, explore every surface, and kiss every inch of her.

He lifted his head and looked down at her. Her face was flushed and soft, her mouth parted, her eyes just gleaming slits of blue between dark lashes. He couldn't resist kissing her again and again, until he heard her moan softly, until he tasted the tang of blood on her lower lip.

"Mary," he said with a gasp, lifting his head and pressing her cheek to his chest. "Oh, doll, I hurt you." He felt her shake her head in denial.

"I did," he murmured. "And I'm sorry. It just got out of hand."

She sighed, slid her arms from around his middle up to encircle his neck, and pulled him down to her. "I . . . like . . . kisses that . . . get out of . . . hand," she whispered between pecks. "And for some strange reason, I don't feel the least bit . . . alarmed anymore. I feel . . ." She let it trail off as she gazed at him with such astonishment, he nearly choked on the lump in his throat. Thank heaven, he wasn't in this all alone!

"Oh, sweetheart!" Elation leapt within him. She wanted him as much as he wanted her. His knee slid between hers, his arms wound tightly around her slender body. He could feel her thighs squeezing his leg, the press of her breasts against his chest, the pounding of her heart echoed in her throat. "What do you feel?" he murmured against the warm skin of her neck.

"That this is happening too fast . . . and yet not fast enough." Mary was astonished at her sudden ability to say exactly what she felt to this man.

"I know," he said, lifting his head and smiling down at her. "It's that way for me too. We need to stop, catch our breath, think a little, don't we? Sort out our feelings before we get caught up in them and blown . . . right . . . away." He couldn't, he discovered, leave her lips alone.

"Yes." She kissed him again, a deep, drawing kiss that left him reeling. He was grateful for the couch at the backs of his knees as he collapsed downward, scooping her onto his lap. "We should slow down," she added with an ecstatic sigh, going full steam ahead, nibbling at his throat, his earlobes, the point of his chin.

"I know." His thumb slid across the tip of her shoulder, moving aside the lapel of her robe. There was no strap of a nightgown to block his way, and his heart lurched inside his chest. *Oh, Lord! She's naked! Give me strength!*

"You shouldn't be touching me like that, if . . . we're going to slow down," she said in a soft sigh. "I should make you stop."

"Make me stop." His voice was thick, almost unintelligible.

"Okay, I will, in a . . . minute." She shuddered as

his palm slid down over a breast, and then she cried out softly, arching herself into his clasp. "Oh, Bruce . . ."

"Mary, I want you. Oh, love, I want you so much."

Her head fell back on his shoulder as he parted the front of her robe and bent his head to kiss the swelling curves there. He felt the deep, shuddering breath that convulsed her, heard her moan of pleasure, and opened his mouth to taste the sweetness of her breast for the first time. The hardness of her nipple burst against his tongue, and he groaned, sucking her deeply into his mouth. Her hands tangled in his hair, pressing his mouth harder against her. She sobbed out a word that might have been a plea for more, or a plea for him to stop.

He cupped her other breast, moved his mouth over to it, and was rewarded by her easing into a better position for him to reach her. Her hand slid up the inside of his sweatshirt, nails lightly raking his back, and then smoothing over his skin. "So good, so good," she murmured. "Bruce, it feels so good!"

"To me, too, love," he said, running his hands around her back inside her robe, lifting her higher, licking her nipples. "Oh, Mary, why did it take me so many years to find you? I've wasted so much of my life!"

He scooped her up, then swung her around on the couch, leaning over her, pressing hot kisses to her mouth again. "I'm going to love you like I've never loved any other woman, Mary. I'm going to make you so happy, fill you with my love, give you everything you've ever dreamed of, take you places you've never been before and—Where are you going?"

"The doorbell is ringing. Bruce, there's someone at the door."

"No, ignore it, forget it, whoever it is will go away," he murmured against her throat, his hand sliding lower, getting caught where her sash fastened her robe.

"Bruce, stop!" she said urgently, pushing him up as someone knocked at the door and rang the bell again.

"Sit up, for heaven's sake! It's Mr. Taylor!"

"Oh, hell!" Bruce sat up and pulled his shirt down. "Dammit! The man has the lousiest timing I've ever heard of!"

"I know. But . . ." She drew in a breath, looking at him, her eyes full of pain and sorrow and regret. And love? he wondered, not certain he would recognize it in her if it were there. Was this the way it really happened after all? Out of the blue? Without either person knowing what they were supposed to do, how they were supposed to respond. Hell, he knew how to respond, all right! But the question remained, what was he responding to? A beautiful woman? Or . . . *the* woman?

He caught her hands and held her before him, his eyes burning into hers while the impatient knocking went on and on. "But what? But you're glad we were interrupted?"

She said nothing, just looked at him as if she didn't know the answer, and he had to let her go. Her face was pale except for two bright flags of color high on her cheekbones. Her eyes were dark, almost indigo.

Mary turned from him, tightened the sash of her bathrobe, and opened the door for the super.

He stood there, filling the entire doorway, red toolbox in his hand, brows raised as he looked from Mary's set face to Bruce's expressionless one. He smirked at the sight of the pillow strategically placed on Stud's lap, switched his grin to Mary's pink cheeks, and said, "I heard your door was stuck. I see you got inside all right, though."

"Yes." It was all she could do to speak.

"It's about time you got here," said Stud with a sudden surge of fury. "And a good thing I came to let Miss DeLaney back in. She could have died of hypothermia waiting for you out there in the rain."

"She doesn't look chilled to me," said Taylor as he waddled across the room. "Overheated, I'd say. But then, it is July, rainy day or not." He set the box down and crouched, looking like a large toad, peering into the track the door ran in. "Rain isn't all that cold in July."

He received no response from either of his tenants, shrugged, then grunted and attended to his chore. He shook the door a few times, made it slide another inch or two, then grunted again. He took a can of spray from his toolbox, aimed the nozzle at the groove under the door, and sprayed liberally, all the while rocking the glass panel. In moments it was freed up and sliding smoothly.

"There you go," he said, capping the spray can and heaving himself to his feet with much groaning and straining. "That ought to hold it for now. I'll come in with a buffer and polish up that slot in a day or two. Have fun, kiddies." He gave them both a speculative look, smiled to himself, and lumbered out.

As the door closed, Mary sighed almost silently and went to stand at the balcony door, gazing out over the wet courtyard.

Bruce came up behind her and put his hands on her shoulders. "You okay?"

She nodded but said nothing

"Are you sorry?"

Again, she nodded.

"About what? About our being stopped? Or about our getting started in the first place?"

She turned then, looking at him, her blue eyes dark with something he couldn't name. "Bruce, it shouldn't have gone that far. I apologize for leading you on. But I don't have flings. I don't indulge in casual sex. And commitment is not something—" She broke off. It wouldn't be fair to state that she knew he wasn't looking for commitment, because maybe it wasn't true, but what he had said about the teacher back in Manitoba had certainly led her to consider that as a possibility. Maybe, as he'd said, he simply didn't want to share his life with *Evelyn*. Still, it was far too early in their relationship for her to start thinking along those lines. "We really don't know each other very well," she finished lamely.

It was almost a question, Stud thought. One she was too polite to ask, having once asked and received an evasive answer. She was offering him an opportunity to talk to her, tell her about himself and his job, especially now that it was established that it wasn't what she'd thought. He drew in a deep breath, wanting to tell her but knowing exactly what would happen if he did. She'd throw him out before he had even half a chance to make her see reason. Once they were closer, once they had developed mutual trust, knew more about each other, maybe then he could find a gentle way to tell her, a way that wouldn't send her off the deep end. So he put his painful conscience into the back of his mind, closed the lid on it, and concentrated on this new and exciting relationship he could feel developing between them. It was—he more than just suspected—a far more important relationship than any other he'd been part of, and as for her unwillingness to make a commitment, he was sure he could overcome that in time. All it would take was careful planning, teamwork. Trouble was, he didn't have a team to work with anymore. All he had was himself. And Mary. He smiled. And what a team they were going to make!

"Making love is one excellent way for two people to get to know each other," he pointed out with great logic. "But you're right. If we had continued on that path, it would have been because we got carried away by our own excitement, not because we had both made a reasoned decision and agreed logically that it was the right thing for us both. So for that reason I'm not as sorry as I might be that we were interrupted."

She remembered his saying, over the Chinese dinner they'd shared, that he preferred the team approach to things, decisions made in advance, so that everyone knew what to do and when to do it, even in the excitement of the game.

Mary sighed again, and he thought it was a sigh of relief. Reaching up, she stroked his face with the palm of her hand. Her skin was so soft, he was afraid his beard stubble would damage it. Funny, he hadn't worried about that when he'd been kissing her earlier. But then, he hadn't even been capable of coherent thought.

"Did I say thanks for rescuing me?"

He grinned, captured her hand, and turned his lips against it. "As a matter of fact, you didn't. All you did was abuse me for not being Mr. Taylor."

She tugged her hand free and returned to the center of the living room, sinking down onto the edge of a chair. "Not true. I was annoyed with you for not getting him to come up. I was wrong about that, too, wasn't I? You did try, but he was all wrapped up in his shows."

He followed her, leaning one shoulder on the mantel of the small gas fireplace. "That's right." He grinned and ran a hand into his hair, leaving it sticking up. "But I have to confess I could have tried harder." He crossed the room to crouch before her, taking her hands in his. "Tell me, what were you doing out there in the rain in the first place, wearing . . . next to nothing?" His eyes, warm and insinuating, swept over her terry robe, lingering on her breasts, reminding her of the way they had swept over her wet nightgown. Her heart hammered slowly, and her breath seemed caught up somewhere just below her throat. Under the intensity of his gaze, she felt her nipples tighten and pucker almost painfully. One of his hands slipped to the inside of her knee, stroking lightly where her bathrobe was parted.

"I couldn't get to sleep," she murmured, fighting

now to keep her eyes open. Her lids felt heavy, her lungs couldn't get enough oxygen, and it had absolutely nothing to do with the need for rest. "Bruce . . . don't touch me like that."

"Like what? Like this?" The thumb of his left hand traced the curve of her calf down to her ankle and back up again. "What kept you awake?"

"I don't . . . know. Maybe too much . . . coffee at work."

"Maybe," he agreed. "But maybe not." He looked up at her. "Right?"

She sighed again—a short, tremulous sound—and he stilled his hand on her leg, feeling a fine tremor in her muscles. "Maybe."

"I had a hard time getting to sleep too."

"Oh." Without her permission, her right hand reached out, one finger extended, and traced one side of his mustache, from midpoint along its straight part, and then down the sharp curve toward his chin. She then traced the other side of it, her finger lingering on the silken hairs. One of her thumbs accidentally brushed over his lower lip. He shuddered, and drew in a sharp breath. Mary stared at his lips for a long moment before she spoke again. "I think you better go now, desperado," she whispered.

His eyes were full of regret. "I know. I will. We both need some sleep."

He brushed his lips lightly over hers, then got to his feet and went to the door.

"Friends," he said. "It's important that we be friends, Mary, that we like each other as well as—" He broke off with a small, self-conscious shrug.

She nodded, and when the door had closed behind him, she got to her feet and staggered into her bedroom. She shucked her robe, slid into bed without bothering with a nightie, pulled the covers up to her shoulders, and was asleep in an instant.

• • •

The same smile she'd carried with her to bed was on her lips when she awoke, but as she lay there, hands behind her head, thinking over the events of the day, it faded.

Bruce still hadn't told her what he did for a living. Why did he continue to be so evasive? The only conclusion she could draw was that he simply didn't want her getting that involved in his life, that he would, if he could, keep her in one compartment, his work in another.

That hurt. It really did. How could a man kiss her until she had about as much substance left as a cloud, tell her they were going to be not only friends but lovers as well, then keep at least half his life secret from her? She rolled out of bed, got into the shower, and stood there for a long time.

Okay, if that was the way he wanted it, she couldn't do a lot about it. But she would most definitely keep their relationship at the level of friendly companions, and that would be all, thank you very much. All.

She was able to put her new resolve to the test the very next afternoon when Bruce came knocking on her door, a piece of matted dark brown wool over his arm, and a puzzled look on his face. Involuntarily she smiled, and her heart jumped crazily at the sight of him.

This was not, she knew, going to be easy. But she'd keep the man at arm's length until he opened up to her.

Seven

"Hi," she said, stepping back automatically. He followed her inside, leaning against the door with one shoulder until it shut. She thought about telling him to leave, that she had work to do. It wouldn't have been a lie, but it would have been a cop-out. She was fully aware of her body's reaction to his nearness, but who was in charge of things here, her mind or her body? Her mind, of course. For the moment she would let him stay. After all, maybe he'd come to tell her about his job.

"What do you think caused this?" he asked, not bothering with a greeting. He held the brown wool up by its shoulders. It was a very small sweater that had likely once been very large.

"Um . . . a mommy sweater and a daddy sweater sort of . . . well, got together?" she asked solemnly.

He gave her a dirty look. "Not one hour ago," he said indignantly, "this sweater fit me."

"I see. And you washed it, right?"

"Right."

"In hot water, right?"

He looked triumphant. "Wrong! I remember my mother and sisters washing sweaters," he said. "Cold water, hand wash, the works."

"Dryer?"

"Dryer . . . ?" he asked hollowly.

Mary nodded. "What did the instructions say about drying?"

"There's supposed to be instructions about drying the damn thing?"

Mary laughed. "As a rule." She reached out and took the sweater from him, and when their hands touched, she felt as if an electric charge had gone through her. Her breath caught in her throat. She backed up quickly, studying the little tag in the neck of the sweater, fighting for control. This was ridiculous! She couldn't go into heart failure just because she'd touched his hand, for heaven's sake!

"What can I do about it?" he asked, stepping closer, and her gaze flew to his face. Do about what? Her incipient heart failure? Back up is what he could do about it!

"N-nothing," she said.

"Can't fix it, huh?" He reached to take the sweater back from her, and managed to capture her hand in his at the same time. Gently, but inexorably, he pulled her toward him until their bodies touched.

She shook her head, her eyes on the level of his collarbone, her breath hung up on the level of her own. "No," she said. "It can't be fixed at all. Do you . . . do you know any needy midgets?"

There was silence for several seconds, then he tilted her chin up with one fist. "I know one needy man."

She stepped away from him. "I'm sure. I hope it will fit him. How's work?"

Her words slammed into him. He had to tell her. That was all there was to it. He just had to sit down and do it. He'd never known that anything could be so hard, though. This was the worst situation he could possibly imagine. He was in love with a woman who was going to hate what he did for a living and was probably going to hate him—one, for not telling her at the very outset, and two, for doing the damned job in the first place. He tried to smile but knew it was a travesty. "Fine," he said. "How's yours?"

It was impossible not to feel disappointed. She'd given him the perfect opening, and he'd evaded her again. "Okay," she said stiffly, "but I have a lot to do today."

He couldn't deny the wave of relief that washed over him. "No time for a cup of coffee with me?" He didn't want to have coffee with her. He wanted to get out of there before his conscience made him tell her the truth and her conscience made her say she couldn't see him again.

"I . . . No. No, I have too much to do." She passed the sweater back to him, opened the door. "I'm sorry. Good-bye, Bruce."

He balled up the sweater in his hand, tossing it up and catching it, looking at her, his eyes full of unspoken questions and something else she couldn't get a handle on. It seemed, she thought, that he was glad she was kicking him out, that his asking for coffee had only been a polite gesture, something completely opposite to what he wanted. If she'd said yes, would he suddenly have remembered a previous engagement?

"Okay," he said, smiling now, confirming her suspicions. It was, if ever there had been, a smile of total relief. "See you soon."

"Yes, sure," she murmured. "Soon."

But it wasn't soon. It wasn't soon at all. Mary watched three days go by, then four, then five. She found herself sighing for no good reason at all, and staring off into space. Bruce, it seemed, didn't want to be her friend. He didn't want to bother giving her the chance to get to know him before dragging her into bed. At that she almost smiled. If he showed up on her doorstep, she might be the one to drag him into bed, given the way she was feeling, and to hell with the consequences. She thought about calling him, about going to his door on some pretext or other. But what? She had never chased a man in her life and didn't know how to begin. No, all she could do was wait and see if he would come to her. She knew it wasn't supposed to be that way anymore, that women could go after what they wanted just as easily as men could, that many men actually preferred it. Something told her, though, that Bruce Hagendorn wouldn't be one of those men, and she forced herself to remember the relief in his eyes when she'd refused to have a cup of coffee with him that last day she'd seen him. Maybe the reason he'd come to her apartment then was to tell her that he had plenty of friends now and didn't need her anymore. He could have intended to sit down with her, explain himself, and then bow out of her life, and was relieved when she rushed him through the door, because it meant he could just fade out of her life instead.

The only trouble was, she didn't want him to bow out of her life, or fade out either, and the only way he could know that was if she told him. Still, she couldn't make herself do it. But on the other hand she wasn't going to sit around waiting for him to make a move. No way. She was getting on with her life, going to work, going to the university, planning her upcoming vacation. Sure she was. The most productive decision she'd made about that damned vacation was *not* to let Kevin's parents know she was taking one.

Maybe, Mary finally decided when more than a week had gone by without Bruce appearing at her door, he, too, sensed that a casual friendship would be too hard to maintain. Several times she'd sneaked out onto her balcony to see if he was in his pool, but she'd never seen him. It hurt, missing him so. She had wanted never to hurt like this again.

So when he spoke right behind her on Thursday morning as she entered her apartment, saying, "Hi. Can I come in?" she nearly dropped her keys and her laundry basket, couldn't catch her breath for several seconds, then felt a massive surge of rage. He'd put her through *hell* for over a week, and now he just casually, nonchalantly, wanted to *come in*?

She whirled around, glaring at him, and shook her hair back from her face. "No!"

He was wearing a crumpled pink shirt with short sleeves, a pair of tan rugby pants, and unlaced sneakers with no socks. His face looked pale, worn, and stubbly, as if he hadn't been asleep yet after his late evening at work. But then, she thought, she must look much the same, with the exception of the stubble. She hadn't been asleep yet, either, and she'd worked a lot more hours than he had.

"No," she said curtly. "I was just on my way to bed."

Her eyes were intensely blue, hard, and angry. "I've missed you," he said softly.

Her expression never changed. Only her chin tilted a fraction of an inch higher. "I've been here."

He didn't blame her. He owed her an explanation. Several, probably. "I really wanted to talk to you. All this time I've wanted to come and see you, but—" He broke off, gnawing at his lower lip.

"It's all right. I understand. Now that you're settled in your job, you have lots of new friends, and you don't need me any longer. That's fine. I don't need you either."

He drew in a deep breath and said, "I do need you. I want to be with you."

She felt herself begin to soften. He did look awful. "Is something wrong?" she asked.

He hesitated, and then nodded. "My grandmother died."

"Oh, Bruce!" She set her basket down on the floor, shut the door, and hugged him warmly, wondering dimly how in the world they had both gotten inside her apartment without her noticing. "I'm sorry. What a sad time this must be for you."

He held her tightly, seeming to take comfort in her presence, and she let him for several minutes before leading him to the sofa. "Come on," she said. "Sit down.

"Are you going home? Can I call and book you a flight?"

"No," he said, leaning his head on the back of the couch, his eyes closed, his fingers linked tightly with hers. "I just wanted to be with you for a while. I know you haven't slept yet, so I won't keep you long."

"That's okay," she said. "I'm happy to be here for you. But won't your family expect you to go home?"

Even with his eyes shut he looked uncomfortable. "No."

"I see." She didn't. Surely they could forgive him at least enough to share their grief with him? "Want to talk about it?" she invited.

"There's not a lot to talk about," he said, lifting his head and smiling down at her, tracing her cheek with the tip of one finger. "I heard the elevator stop on your floor and just felt lonely all of a sudden, thinking of you up here and me down there. I thought maybe you'd be a bit lonely, too, because we haven't seen each other for a long time."

And wasn't that the truth! Lonely hardly covered it. She got to her feet, wanting something to do, not wanting to look at him, show him all she was feeling. "Do you . . . do you want some coffee?"

"Sure!" There was relief in his voice, and she was glad she'd let him come in. She knew what it was like to grieve all alone. Oh, there had been plenty of people around her, but no one who was really capable of alleviating her grinding sense of aloneness. If she could do that for just one other human being, then her life would have been well spent. *Oh, pooh!*

she said to herself, *such a highfalutin motive! Face it. You want Bruce here. You've missed him too much.*

"That is, if you have time and you aren't too tired," Bruce added, seeing her swallow a yawn.

"I'm fine," she assured him with a smile. "We had a surprisingly easy night, and I have no classes today."

He followed her into the kitchen and sat down at the table watching her make the brew. Now was the time to tell her. All he had to do was say, *Mary, listen to me. I have something to say that you're not going to like, but if we care about each other as much as I think we do, then we can work it out.* Sure. Hadn't he spent over a week rehearsing what he was going to tell her? Of course he had. Well, today was the day. Now was the time. He opened his mouth and spoke.

"I like the way you move your hands. They look like little ballerinas dancing."

Mary glanced at him, startled, bemused. She felt a laugh bubble up in her chest. "Ballerinas?" She transferred her gaze to her hands for a moment. To her they looked just like hands. She tried to imagine them wearing little tulle skirts, maybe toe shoes on the fingers.

"Yeah. You know, dainty, graceful, but lively. Sort of . . . efficient too." He wondered how they were going to feel strangling him.

"Thanks." She smiled and sat down across from him, feeling suddenly self-conscious about her hands, not quite knowing what to do with them. She folded them on the table in front of her. Bruce covered them with one of his.

"I want to talk to you." His voice was hoarse. "But it's not easy."

"I know, but it will help if you talk about her," she said compassionately. "You said once that your grandmother had helped to raise you. Tell me about that, Bruce," she said, deftly sliding her hands out from under his, putting them in her lap and clenching them together. His touch, as casual as it had been, set up too loud a clamor in her blood. "Your mother's mother, or your father's?"

He sighed, shook his head, and looked down at the table. Then, with a shrug, he said, "My mother's. She lived with us on the farm. My other grandmother died before I was born. But Grandma . . . she was an essential part of life to me. She practically raised us single-handedly, because Mom spent so much time out in the fields working with Dad. I loved her more than I loved anyone else, I think."

His smile was reminiscent as he warmed to the subject. "She was the littlest thing you've ever seen. About five feet nothing, when my mom was growing up, but then she shrank, I guess, because by the time I was ten and had reached four feet nine, we were the same height. But boy, did she pack a wallop for a tiny old lady!"

Mary raised her brows. She didn't try to hide her amusement at the idea of Bruce being spanked. "She walloped you?"

"Only when I needed it." He was looking less weary, more relaxed. He even smiled a bit.

"Like when?"

"Oh . . ." He thought for a moment or two, then said, "Like the time I got two small inner tubes, tied net in them, and told Tracy if she stood in them, she'd be able to walk all the way across the dugout."

Mary looked perplexed. "Walk across a canoe? Why?"

He snorted. "'Not a canoe! On the prairies a dugout's a man-made pond. Anyway, I wasn't sure it would work, and didn't want to try it myself, so I sent Tracy. Of course, her feet kept lifting out of the tubes whenever she took a step, so I tied her shoes to the nets. She fell, naturally, and there she was, floating feet up, head down, about to drown when Grandma heard me hollering. She dove in and dragged Tracy out, made sure she was all right, then paddled me within an inch of my life."

Mary grinned. "She didn't even have to ask whose idea the stunt was, did she?"

"Nope. And then there was the time she baked a chocolate cake for the church bazaar, threatened long and difficult death to anyone who touched it, and went out to pick vegetables for dinner. I wanted that cake so bad! It just about killed me thinking someone who didn't want it as much as I did was going to buy it and eat it. I couldn't let it go to the church."

"So? How did you get that cake?"

He sighed. "I didn't. But I sure got a licking. I opened the back door, sprinkled oats across the yard, up the steps, across the porch, and into the kitchen. Along came a Banty hen, just as I'd planned, into the house, up onto a chair—with only a little help—and then onto the table, where she made a wonderful mess of Grandma's icing. I was so proud of myself! Of course, she wasn't going to take any old chicken-pecked cake to the church! Only the best went to bazaars, so we'd get to keep that cake at home and eat it. Everyone, even Grandma, was going to be pleased about that come dessert time." He frowned, shook his head.

"And Grandma came in, saw you watching the chicken with a devilish grin on your face, and gave you exactly what you deserved. And no cake."

He looked at her in amusement. "Yup, you know just the way things are supposed to go. You'll make a hell of a mother, Mary, and a grand—" He half-rose. "Mary? What is it?"

"What's what?" Her voice sounded dim.

He sat back down. "Your face went dead white for a minute. Are you okay?"

"I'm fine. Nothing wrong with my color. Must be the light in here." She jumped up, got two cups from a cupboard, the sugar bowl from another, and the milk from the refrigerator, and set them on the counter. Her hands shook. She struggled to steady herself.

"You miss your own grandmother, don't you?"

She leapt at that. "Yes. Of course."

"Maybe I shouldn't talk about mine."

"It's all right. Go on. Tell me more about growing up wild on the prairies." She returned and sat down.

"Hell," he laughed. "We weren't allowed to be wild. We were disciplined from day one. Farm kids normally are, you know. There's so much potential danger, they have to be. Parents get very upset when their kids get themselves killed."

The coffeepot gurgled. The aroma floated through the kitchen. Stud watched the color ebb from Mary's face once more, saw the awful, frozen smile she kept aimed at him, and knew there was something terribly wrong. "Ah, doll," he said, getting up, touching her cool skin. "What is it? Something's hurting you. Are you sick?"

"No."

"Then . . . what I said. It brought back some kind of pain you've felt. Tell me, Mary. Please."

She rose again. "The coffee's ready. Want some, or do you want to go home?"

"In other words shut up and drink my coffee, or get out?" he asked, astounded.

She poured without answering, set a cup before him, and then filled one for herself, remaining at the counter, her back to him.

"Someday will you tell me about it?" he persisted, watching as she stirred sugar into her coffee. Her slim shoulders were tense under her green T-shirt. "Mary?"

She shook her head. "I can't . . . talk about it. Sorry. Every time I do, I cry."

He swallowed very hard several times before he said, "I could hold you while you cry. It might make it easier if you did talk about it. That's what you just told me, and I believe it. Maybe the tears would wash away some of the pain."

She shook her head again, her brown hair rippling on her shoulders. She shoved her fingers into the hip pockets of her jeans. He saw that her hands were shaking. "Nothing washes away that kind of pain," she said huskily. "It just . . . lives there. Forever."

He wanted to go to her, touch her, turn her into his arms and comfort her. But something told him not to. Not now. Not this time. She wouldn't want his touch. Maybe, though, words would help.

"No, love. Not forever. I promise you that. It does get better. When more time has passed, you'll be able to see that. Right now the wound is too fresh," he said, having no idea if he was right or wrong, just hoping to provide some small comfort to her.

"Four years," she told him raspily, taking her hands out of her pockets, gripping the edge of the sink, staring out at the wall of windows in the building across the way. "I should be over it. I should be healing."

"That's not long. I remember when Grandma first died. I was nearly fourteen. I couldn't even look at a picture of her without breaking down. And for quite a few years I couldn't bear to talk about her, either, but that—"

She whirled around, her face full of accusations. He rolled his eyes heavenward and clapped his hand over his mouth.

"What? What did you say?"

"Oh, hell," he muttered. "Caught." He flung his hands out in a gesture of surrender. "So go ahead. Hang me, torture me. Throw me to the alligators. Pound me with a frying pan. That's what *she* would have threatened. Any or all of those and a few more besides."

"You," she said, coming to stand over him, hands on hips, "are a brat. But I've commented on that before, haven't I?" He was glad, so glad, to see that the shadows had gone from her eyes, that they danced now with small lights of amusement.

"I guess so." He somehow managed to look properly contrite. "I'm sorry, doll. I didn't really mean to lie to you, but you were being so cold and angry out there in the hall, and when you asked me if something was wrong, I figured you'd let me in if you thought there was a problem. And since Grandma's death was the worst thing that's ever happened to me, that was what came to mind." He snatched at her hand, caught her wrist, and spun her around so she sat on his lap. "And I was telling the truth when I said I was lonely for you."

She sighed and nodded her head. "Yes. I know. I've been lonely, too, Bruce."

"Lonely for me?" he asked hopefully.

"Yes. For you." Her eyes were so blue, he felt as if he could have sailed in their depths.

"So why didn't you come and knock on my door? Or call me on the phone?"

She swallowed hard. "I wanted to. I just didn't know how. Why did you stay away so long?"

"Mary . . . sweet Mary." He cradled her against him, tucking her head onto his shoulder, reveling in the scent of her hair, the softness of her skin, the warmth of her body. He wanted to kiss her, but didn't dare; the moment was too precious. It needed to be savored, treasured. He was about to take the biggest risk in his life, telling her about his new business. And when she knew, there was at least an eighty percent chance, he figured, that she'd toss him off her balcony. So, for now, he'd hold her. It might be his last opportunity.

Mary leaned on him, her eyes closed, enjoying this closeness for just a few minutes. He stroked her hair, her shoulder, her back. She felt her body relaxing, softening, molding itself to his shape, and knew she had to move. She couldn't stay like this with him. It wasn't fair to either of them, yet she had no strength to pull away.

"I'm so tired," she murmured. "So sleepy. Go home, Bruce. I need to go to bed."

"I love to hold you," he said, his voice a deep rumble. "I love to feel you against me. Know what I want to do this minute?"

She had to laugh, as tired as she was. It was a soft, breathless little sound. "I can guess," she said, because she was sure that what he wanted was exactly what she wanted—in spades.

He smacked her thigh gently, then stroked his hand all the way down to her knee and back up again. "Not that. Strangely enough at this minute that's not what I want. What I want is to lie down on your bed with you, and hold you while we both sleep."

Her sigh was ragged. After a long moment she said in a barely audible voice, "I'd like that too."

"But," he said, tilting her face up so he could see her expression, the darkening in his eyes reflecting the turbulence of his thoughts, "trouble is, we'd wake up. In time we'd wake up, and maybe just holding you wouldn't be enough then."

She swallowed the hard lump in her throat. "I know." She lifted her hand and cupped it around his jaw, liking the rasp of his whiskers against her palm. It was such an intimate feeling, and it felt somehow right. "You know, Bruce, at this moment I don't think I care what might happen in five or six hours. I want you to lie down with me and hold me, let me hold you." She felt tears of weakness, of weariness fill her eyes and blinked them back. Two trickled over anyway. He caught them on his fingertip, looked at them, then at her. There were questions in his eyes, questions she wasn't ready to answer.

"Bruce, I don't like being lonely," she whispered.

"I don't want to be lonely anymore. But I don't know if . . ."

He stood, still holding her, and carried her into her bedroom. "It's all right. I understand." He sat her down on the edge of the bed, took off her shoes, and lifted her legs up. Kicking off his own shoes, he lay beside her and gathered her close.

"Sleep," he commanded softly. "And lie still," he added as she tightened her arms around him, moved her legs slightly.

Mary felt a huge sob rising up from the pit of her stomach, but before it could force its way out, it somehow transformed itself into a deep, contented sigh, and she slept, deeper and more securely than she'd slept for a long, long time.

She awoke to find herself still wrapped tightly in Bruce's arms, his cheek against the top of her head, his left hand cupping one of her breasts. His warm breath stirred her hair, making it tickle her temple, and she carefully lifted a hand to brush the hair away.

He sighed and shifted, sliding down so that his cheek was on her shoulder. His hand tightened on her breast, and he squeezed it gently, even though he still slept.

A slow, heavy heat began to build in her, rising up her legs to center between her thighs, coiling from her breasts to her belly to curl and pulsate deep within. "Bruce," she whispered. "Wake up."

He opened his eyes and lifted his head. With one finger he traced the outline of her mouth. "Are you real or am I dreaming you again?"

The heat stirred and roiled inside her. She shifted against him, knowing there was no relief in that but only added torture. It was a torture she welcomed. Her breathing grew labored. "I think I'm real. Why don't you kiss me and find out for yourself?"

Slowly he slid his body away from hers, his hand from her breast. She missed his warmth immediately. He rose up until he kneeled on the bed, looking down at her, not touching. "Is that what you want, Mary?"

She nodded. "You're what I want." With a tiny smile she added, "I'm making a reasoned decision, Bruce."

But in spite of her words, he continued to kneel there, his gaze never leaving her face. With unhurried grace she sat up, lifted her T-shirt over her head, and set it aside. She unhooked her bra, slipped its straps down her arms, and dropped it atop the shirt.

Bruce drew in a sharp breath and reached out a hand to touch her. She shuddered at the contact of his fingertips on the underside of her breast. Her nipples puckered and grew taut. "Please," she whispered. "Please make love with me now."

"Yes, oh, yes," he said, pulling her up against him. Cupping her face in his hands, he kissed her, hard and deep and long. She clung to him, soft sounds coming from her throat, her hands sneaking beneath his pink shirt to trace his muscles with curled fingers and lightly raking nails. She wrapped her fingers around his wrists, feeling the strength there, then slid them up over his forearms, loving the roughness of the dark, curling hair. Under his short sleeves her hands moved over his shoulders until the tightening of the fabric prevented further exploration. Twisting free of his seeking mouth, she attacked his buttons, popping them open one by one.

He lifted her chin and looked deeply into her eyes, reading there the truth he had longed to see. Leaning forward, he gently guided her back down to the mattress, laying her flat, his big body hard and heavy on hers. With one hand slipped between their two heated bodies, he found her breast and massaged it, rolling the hard nipple against his palm as she arched into him. Against her lower body she felt the pulsating hardness of his arousal, and she ached with need, longed for the strength to beg him to fulfill the promise his desire was making, but she couldn't breathe, let alone talk. She gasped again, but the weight of him compressed her chest. A swirling dizziness came over her. The air was filled with the scent of their bodies, the heavy musk of desire, the sound of their harsh breathing. It was a primitive sound, a primitive scent, a primitive need she was experiencing—and it was the most exciting thing that had ever happened to her. His mouth was driving her insane, his hand on her breast was something she had longed for, his body atop hers a benison long denied, and she welcomed it—him—with every gasping breath she took.

He lifted up, tore off his shirt, and placed his chest against her sensitized nipples. The wealth of dark hair there abraded them. She moaned as he clasped her hips and drew her tightly against him. But their clothing was unbearably constricting. Swiftly he stood up, shucked his crumpled pants, fumbled in the pocket for his wallet, and opened that. Mary smiled, unsnapped her own jeans, and lifted her hips to slide them down, readying herself even as he readied himself for her.

And then he was holding her again, stroking her bare skin, teasing the sensitive insides of her thighs until she was moaning and writhing with need. It was that frantic hunger of hers, the almost frenzied lack of control that gave him pause. He remembered the grief she had refused to discuss. She had loved, that he knew, but when? And who? And . . . how often?

Gently he tried to soothe her, calm her, but she moved against him with such a fierce excitement that he had to leash his own need with greater willpower than he'd ever been called on to exercise before. Desperately he wanted to dive deeply into her, claim her, fill her with himself, quench that fire of hers that was all but consuming them both. Instead, he held her away for a moment, looking at her, shaking her slightly to get her attention.

"Darling, wait. I have to know. How long has it been for you?"

She turned a delicate shade of pink but continued to meet his gaze. "Too long, Bruce. Please, hurry!"

"If it's been too long, we mustn't hurry. I want you ready, love."

"I am, I am, but it's been four years. More than that. Come into me," she cried softly, parting her legs and wrapping them around his hips. "I need you now, Bruce. I do."

"Yes, love. Soon," he promised, his fingers making soft, sliding motions as he discovered her shape, her heat, her slick desire. "I don't want to hurt you." He sucked on her nipples, kissed her mouth, and then levered himself over her, probing gently until he was just at her entrance. She squeezed her eyes shut, cried softly that she needed him. He had to know who she needed. "Mary, open your eyes. Look at me. Know me."

She understood. No ghosts in this bed. No past. Only now, the present, Bruce and her together. It had to be this way. She looked at him from glazed eyes. "Bruce, I want you."

Slowly, with infinite care, he moved into her, his large body trembling with the effort of holding back for her. "Tight," he whispered. "So tight. So hot. Mary . . ." and then he was fully encased within her flesh, and she surged up against him, caught in a series of spasms that could no more be controlled than could the tide. It was heaven. It was perfection. It was what life meant. He thrust, she caught him, held him, then reluctantly let him go so he could pull out and thrust again. Her internal fire flared out of control, when, like a stately dance gone wild, his movements became rapid, short, determined. He joined in her ecstasy, clasping her tightly to him, pumping into her until they both collapsed, sobbing each other's names. As they slowly came back down to earth they exchanged gentle kisses wherever lips happened to fall.

Somewhere during that period, Mary realized, she must have fallen asleep again, because when she awoke, she found herself tucked neatly under the covers. She laid a hand on the dent in the pillow next to hers. Cool. She smiled as the scent of bacon came floating into the bedroom. Bacon. Bruce.

Bruce cooking? Cooking in her kitchen? Her smile faded, and she leapt out of bed, snatching up her bathrobe from its hook behind the door. She ran out, her imagination telling her she'd better get busy and rescue her kitchen before it was utterly destroyed.

Eight

She was too late, of course. The destruction was complete, and as she stood in the doorway, suddenly feeling shy, she knew that the destruction of her resistance to one ex-hockey player was even more complete. He turned, dropped a spatula onto an already messy stove, and held out his arms. Without hesitation she walked into them, sliding her own around him, clinging tightly.

For a long time she just held him, savoring the moment, savoring memories, savoring dreams of the future. Then, he moved. Encircling her face, he tilted it up, smiling at her with a wealth of tenderness in his eyes, so that she wondered if the dreams were hers alone. "Hi," he said. "Have a good sleep?"

She nodded within the clasp of his hands around her face. "The best. You?"

"Oh, yes," he said, dropping a kiss onto the tip of her nose, another onto her lips, sliding his mouth across her chin and down her throat. "The best . . ." He drew in a tremulous breath and dragged her even closer. "The very best, Mary." And she didn't think he was talking just about sleeping.

Warmth flooded her body again, along with need, deep and abiding. She didn't ever want to have this man leave her. But she still didn't know the rules of his game. "Bruce . . ." She drew in an unsteady breath, touched his cheek with her palm, turning his face back to hers. "Bruce, we have to talk."

"No." With two fingers he covered her lips. "Don't say anything now, love. I agree. We do have things to talk about, and we are going to do it. But first we have to eat. Breakfast is ready."

"But—"

"Please?"

How could she resist a pleading desperado? "Okay." She grinned and stepped away from him. "Considering the mess you've made, this food had better be good, mister."

It was.

They laughed and talked together over their eggs Benedict, arguing amiably about books and movies, political issues and tastes in decor. He had none, she accused. He had, he insisted, he simply hadn't developed it to the fullest yet. He'd bought cushions, hadn't he?

"But," she said, shoving her plate aside, brushing toast crumbs into a heap and placing her elbows on the table, "your idea of patio furniture leaves a lot to be desired." She had to laugh thinking about him and his ridiculous pool. "Where did you get that thing? And why?"

"It was a joke. A friend in Winnipeg had it delivered to me after I'd complained about the awful vacancy rate here, and the fact that I couldn't find a place to rent in a building with a pool. Swimming is my second favorite pastime."

"After hockey?"

He grinned wickedly. "Nope. Not anymore."

She felt herself flush at the sexy expression on his face. "Oh." She looked down, flicked her nail through the toast crumbs, then glanced up at him again. "You can't exactly swim in that pool."

"No, but since it was paid for, I had to accept it,

didn't I? And once I had it, I figured the best thing to do was to use it. Besides, I enjoy it. And it's sure a lot quieter than a real pool would be."

"I thought you didn't like quiet. I thought parties and people and music and noise were your things."

"They are," he said, turning serious. "But I also like solitude, my own space, time to regroup and replenish myself from my inner resources. I prefer a mixture, Mary, a blend of different types of entertainment. People who let themselves get into ruts tend to grow old too soon, to become bored with life and boring to others."

She shot him a pained glance. "Thanks."

He looked startled, then chagrined. "Hey, I didn't mean you. You aren't boring."

"I don't go to many parties. I prefer a quiet life."

"Right now I can see that you need a quiet life. I know your nights at work are far from serene, and I can imagine how hard it must be, studying, working on your thesis, preparing for the seminars you lead, and doing your research. I know you have a heavy load, so of course you need time alone and without any hassles to rebuild your strengths. I wasn't getting at you, doll. I promise."

She relaxed. "Okay. But you wouldn't be the first, if you had been. My friend Aggie is always after me to loosen up, to have more fun, to fool around instead of working all the time. I know she does it because she cares about me, worries about me, but still, it rankles. And I will loosen up," she added. "I've got some vacation time coming. I just haven't decided what to do with it yet."

"You said a while back that you didn't intend to stay working at the detox center forever. How long do you plan to be there?" Maybe if she didn't see the downside of drinking every day, she'd be able to ease up on her attitudes.

"I don't know. My contract's up at the end of September. I'm not sure if I'll renew."

"Don't," he said with a quiet urgency that startled her. "I hate having you work there."

"Bruce, why?"

"Because it's dangerous for one thing, and in a lousy part of town for another, and—" He broke off. "Mary, there's something I have to tell you, and I know you're not going to like it. I know I should have done it a long time ago, but I just couldn't seem to find a way, so I kept putting it off and—"

The doorbell rang long and loud. Mary stood, frowning, torn between wanting to hear what Bruce had to say and wanting to stop the awful racket coming from the other side of the apartment.

"Go ahead," he said. "It'll keep." And, not for the first time, she got the impression he was glad not to have to talk to her about whatever was bothering him. His job, of course. He was about to tell her what he did for a living, and he thought she wouldn't like it. She looked at him, at his set face, his eyes full of misery, and agreed with him silently that she wasn't going to like it. Only . . . why wasn't she?

The bell rang again.

"Oh, Mr. Taylor. Is something wrong?"

"Nope. I just want to run this over the slot for your door so it won't stick again." He held up an electric drill with a steel wool attachment on it. "I waited until I was sure you'd be up for the day. Not too early, am I? Oh! Hi there, Stud." The old man looked sly and winked at Bruce, who stood in the kitchen doorway, one shoulder propped against the frame. "Am I interrupting?"

"Of course not," said Mary evenly. "Bruce and I were just sharing a meal. We both have to go to work soon."

"Sure." The super went about his tasks, then as he unplugged the cord of the drill and wound it up, he looked over his shoulder at Bruce.

"And speaking of work," he said, although no one had been—in fact, with the noise of the drill, no one had been speaking at all—"I was thinkin'. You got a big screen at your place over there on Broadway, haven't you?" Without waiting for a reply, he added, "Thinkin' maybe I'd come on by this evening, catch the exhibition game between the Lions and the Bombers, and you could draw me a few drafts. Long time since I've been to a neighborhood—"

"Sure, Jerry, sure. Come on by. Later. Okay? Won't keep you now, though. I know how busy you must be and . . ."

"—pub," Mr. Taylor continued, oblivious to Bruce's attempts to shut him up and speed him out the door. "Anna and I used to go out regular, once a week. Have a few drinks, talk to a few people, have a few laughs. Got out of the habit after I lost her, though. Maybe I should get back into it now that I got me a real live bartender in the house."

And then, when it was much too late, he opened the door and toddled out. Stud closed it behind the old man, leaned against the panels, and looked sadly at Mary.

The silence was potent with unspoken conflict. She hadn't heard right, Mary told herself. Or Mr. Taylor was wrong. Or Bruce, for some reason she couldn't begin to understand, had lied about his job to the super. She sucked in a breath, opened her mouth to speak, and felt her throat close up. She closed her mouth again.

"Mary. Please don't look at me like that. I can explain," said Bruce in a taut tone, his gaze glued to her face, hoping, praying for a glimmer of understanding, and finding none, finding nothing except deep disillusionment.

"Explain? That you're part owner of a neighborhood pub? As in bar?" she asked, her voice nearly unrecognizable. "Why didn't you tell me? Right from day one you knew how I felt about that. You lied by not telling me! I trusted you. How could you keep something so important from me, especially when it became clear I was . . . we were . . . Oh, Lord! You should have told me!"

"I know that!" he said, his own anguish hoarsening his voice. "I tried so many times to find a way to tell you, but by the time I realized how much it was going to matter that you approve of the way I earn my living, I already knew how much you'd hate what I do."

"Well, you sure have that right . . . bartender." The word was an epithet on her tongue. Her expression was murderous. He felt sick. She looked betrayed. He'd known it was going to be bad, but he'd had no idea it was going to be like this—or that he'd feel so damned much guilt. Suddenly he was afraid that he was about to lose something so important that he didn't know what he'd do if he couldn't persuade her to listen to his side of it.

"Mary, please, love, try to lighten up," he said, attempting a smile that missed its mark entirely. He risked moving forward and touching her. She jerked away as if his hand carried poison. "Your clients' problems aren't my fault. I don't create alcoholics, and you know it. Admit that much, at least."

"Oh, sure," she said, her voice cracking, her face pale, "I admit that, Bruce. You don't necessarily create them. You just cater to them." Her ragged laugh held no humor. "You know, I'd rather you ran an escort service." Her chin wobbled for just an instant before she added, "I'd rather you worked for one!" And then she turned, walking quickly into her bedroom, dismissing him. She closed the door with a finality that hurt his heart.

After a long time he left.

Mary heard the door slam behind him and came out of her bedroom. She wandered through the living room, looked out of the window for a few minutes, then slid open the balcony door. She tiptoed out and looked over the rail, staring down into the wading pool, where only a solitary acacia leaf floated. With a soft sigh she went inside again and into the kitchen.

Picking up a dirty glass, she stared at the orange juice clinging to its sides, felt a huge, ugly pressure building up within her, and gave vent to it by flinging the glass across the room. Then, as if there were someone to answer, she shouted, "How could he do this? How can he do this to me? I hate him! He has no right! That's twice now! Twice! Twice he's left me with a filthy kitchen to clean. . . ."

Then, dry-eyed and furious, she swept up the broken glass, shoved all the dishes into the dishwasher, wiped down the table and counters, and scrubbed the floor. Her shoes rang out as she stomped down the hall, punched the elevator button, and waited, tapping an impatient toe.

The doors slid apart. "Mary . . ."

Reaching in, she pushed the button that said Close Door, and snatched her arm back before it did so. She ran down the stairs and out the door, still hearing Bruce behind her, calling her name. "Mary . . ."

He was there again when she got home at eight A.M. This time she had no choice but to ride up with him, to listen to his spiel, but she did not respond. She stared at the buttons until the door opened on her floor, then got out, still ignoring him.

The next morning she went shopping before coming home, so she arrived at a different time than normally, and mercifully did not have to see him, hear him, smell him. The scent of his after-shave nearly made her choke now.

She managed to evade him for several days in a row until she convinced herself that he'd given up, but every so often he was there, and all she could do was tell him to go away, to leave her alone. Why wouldn't he listen, she wondered. Why did he keep on this way? There were a thousand women—a million, probably—he could have. Did he see her as a challenge?

"What kind of relationship do we have that you won't even talk to me about my work or let me talk to you about it? You're not being fair, Mary." Bruce stood, one hand on the rail, the other on the cinder block wall, barring her passage down the back stairs.

"I don't want to talk to you about your work. Nor do I want a relationship with you. I told you that last week. And I told you the same the week before. Go away, Bruce. Leave me alone. And quit lurking in the stairwell."

He grinned, though the smile never quite reached high enough to erase the signs of strain around his eyes. "I have to lurk in the stairwell. You quit riding the elevator."

She sighed. "Only because you were lurking in *it* all the time. Now, please let me pass. I'll be late for class." In fact, she had no class. She was simply going to spend the afternoon in the library; it was either that or sit on her balcony, gazing at an empty wading pool waiting for a glimpse of its owner. She hated herself for that.

"I could drive you out to the university. Car or bike. Take your pick. And then we'd have time to talk a bit."

She fought down the memory of the way it felt to be behind him on that bike. "No." She put her hand on his wrist, trying to lift it out of the way. It was like a bar of iron. A warm, living bar of iron, tense with hard muscle, rough with crisp hair. Quickly she removed her hand. "Bruce, step aside. We have nothing to discuss."

All at once she saw his temper flare. His mouth formed a hard line, a white ring around it. A muscle leapt in his jaw. His eyes lost every flicker of the golden brown that made them hazel, and green fire flamed there.

"We have a hell of a lot to discuss, Mary DeLaney! For one thing I'm in love with you, and up until the old man opened his mouth at the wrong moment, you were on the verge of admitting the same thing to me. I can't let that pass. I can't let it go. Here's my one chance at happiness, and you think you're going to screw it up by acting like some damn fool prohibitionist? Well, lady, I won't let you do that!"

Mary opened her mouth to reply, but since her brain was still trying to sort out what he'd said, no words formed. It was just as well. He wouldn't have heard through the tirade he was still pouring out.

"Dammit, why won't you give me a break? I'm just doing a job I like, a job I'm good at! That doesn't make me some kind of a pariah to the rest of the world, so why does it to you? Where do you get off condemning me?" he demanded, his eyes glittering, voice booming and echoing in the hollow stairwell.

She had never seen him mad. Even that was exciting, she discovered, as exciting as the knowledge that he felt the same way about her as she did about him. He loved her! Not that the knowledge did her any good, because it couldn't lead to anything. Not now. How could she let herself love a bartender any more than she could have loved a male prostitute? She wanted to shriek at the injustice of life, wanted to pound her head against the cinder block wall, wanted to lean her cheek on Bruce's chest and wrap her arms around him and tell him she loved him too. But he gave her no chance to do any of those things. He clamped his hands tightly on her shoulders and continued.

"Where do you get off acting like my judge and jury, even my executioner?" he asked. "Because that's what you're doing, Mary! If you won't let me be part of your life, you might as well execute me."

She steeled herself against his need, against her own. "I'm not judging you!" she said, all the while knowing that she was. Of course she was. And did she have that right? She didn't know. She'd never been judgmental before, only this time the issue was too close to her heart for her to be objective. "But I do have the right to choose my friends from among people I admire and respect," she continued, trying in vain to shrug off his hands.

"And you don't admire or respect me? Is that it?" He gave her a little shake.

"No, I do not! I can't."

"What's so damn bad about what I do, anyway? Just who do you think you are? Carry Nation? You can't single-handedly close every bar in the city, you know!" He looked as if he were about to drag her into his arms and kiss the living daylights out of her.

Suddenly she wanted that so much, she nearly flung herself into his arms. But instead she put her hands on his chest to push him away. Immediately she was caught up by the feel of his heart pounding hard beneath his ribs and snatched her hands down, clenching her fists at her sides, forcing calm into her voice.

"Bruce, you're entitled to run any business you want, and I'm not trying to close anything down," she said, hoping to reach him with reason, hoping to quell his anger before it spilled over into a different kind of passion, one she knew she'd never be able to resist. "But you have to respect my opinions too. I don't want to be friends with anyone who's involved in something so diametrically opposed to everything I believe in, something that counteracts everything I'm trying to accomplish in my life! I'm out to end people's dependency on alcohol. What you're doing is pandering to their desire to obtain it. Well, that's fine. You have a right to do that, and the law is on your side," she added bitterly. "But you have to accept that I have a right not to want to involve myself with you. Call it a conflict of interests if you want. I do not want to be friends with a pub owner, a . . . a bartender. So, let me go."

"Friends?" he said scathingly. "I think we went a little beyond 'friends' with our last encounter, Mary. We are lovers, dammit, and good ones too!"

"Were!" she said. "Were, not 'are.' And it was a mistake, Bruce. It should never have happened."

"I agree completely," he said, shocking her silly. "I didn't mean for it to happen until after I'd told you. I meant to tell you, Mary, in a different way at a different time."

"What different way? What different time? And how could even the most careful choice of words have made any difference? The fact remains, you're doing something I abhor." He agreed? He thought it was wrong that they had made love?

He rubbed a big hand over his face from his forehead to his chin, then placed his palm on her shoulder again. "I don't know what different way I could have told you. I was working on that. Somehow I was going to tell you in a manner you could understand."

"Bruce, dammit, I'm not stupid. I don't lack understanding. I know perfectly well why you're in the booze business. For profit. You don't give a damn about morality, what's right, what's wrong, how many lives you might be destroying!"

He stared at her. "Profit? Hell, if it was just profits I wanted, I could have become a drug dealer, for pete's sake! How would you feel about that? At least what I'm doing for my profit is legal! And for your information, I'm in what you call the 'booze business' because I like bars, not because I'm out to destroy anybody's life. I like people. I like the atmosphere. We're not running a seedy, downtown rum joint for rummies, you know! The Raven's Nest is a nice, respectable, friendly neighborhood pub, and if anyone gets drunk and disorderly, he's out. In fact, we discourage excessive drinking! And we don't serve anyone who's drunk."

"Oh? And do you keep a little breathalyzer machine behind the bar and test them before you serve them? How do you know that the guy you refuse to serve because he looks a little hammered to you isn't going to get in his car and drive to another bar?"

"I don't know that. I only serve adults, and they're supposed to take responsibility for their own actions. I can't control what my customers do when they leave my establishment."

"That's right. You can't. And thanks to you, drunks are turned loose on the streets and highways, drunks who can ram into the cars of innocent people, kill people's husbands, kill people's babies and—"

She choked to a halt, tears streaming from her eyes, as she wrenched herself free of his hold and laid her forehead against the coarse brick of the stairwell, weeping uncontrollably for the first time in years. "Kevin's dead, Bruce! And Andy! Because of a drunk who was served in a pub."

"Oh, Lord," she heard him say as he stroked her back. "*Your* husband? *Your* baby? Mary, my darling. I didn't know!" She didn't respond to his words or his touch, only struggled alone to control the harsh emotions tearing through her. She was used to being alone, used to fighting the pain by herself. She was surprised to discover arms holding her, a warm body rocking hers, and she tried to fight that, too, but could not; she needed it too much. She drew in a harsh breath and smelled Bruce's scent.

He drew her tightly against him, folding his arms across her back, rocking her from side to side as she accepted his warmth, his caring, his compassion, and managed to take some strength from his comforting. When her weeping eased, he asked, "When, sweetheart?" so softly, so sadly, she was nearly undone again.

She wiped her face with her sleeve, fumbled in her

small shoulder bag for a tissue, and blew her nose. After taking a tremulous breath she was able to answer. "Four years ago. I couldn't—" Her voice cracked, but she went on. "I couldn't avoid him. I don't know if I even saw him coming. He was just suddenly there. A green pickup. He came out of a side street and rammed the passenger side of the car. Kevin died instantly. Andy, our two-year-old, died the next day. The drunk got off, Bruce. He got off completely! Just a license suspension for running a stop sign, but no impaired charge, because his lawyer raised a doubt in the judge's mind that the cop's watch had been right at the time of arrest, so maybe the breath samples weren't taken at the proper intervals. I can't remember exactly how it went, just that it was a technicality to do with that damned 'possibly unreliable' watch.

"He left that courtroom laughing, Bruce. And all I could think of was that I'd never see Kevin or Andy laughing again. And he went across the street with his lawyer and his family into a bar to celebrate."

For several minutes he said nothing, just comforted her with the warmth of his body, the solid wrap of his arms. Presently she put her hands up and clasped his elbows, moving his arms down and away. He tried to hold her again, but she forced him back. "No. Let me go."

"I can't let you go," he said with quiet desperation, not holding her but still blocking her way. "We had something going for us that promised to be good, Mary, better than anything I ever expected to find. How can you let the simple matter of my business life and the way you found out about it cancel out all the great stuff we had going for us?"

She couldn't believe that now that she'd told him, he didn't understand. "It isn't a simple matter of a business," she said. "It's an entire lifestyle. And it wouldn't have made a difference who told me what you do for a living, or when I learned it. What we had was gone the minute I knew. Your running a bar is not something I can accept."

"Why not?" he asked impatiently. "Look at it this way: If I wasn't running that bar with Jake, then someone else would be, maybe someone who wouldn't be as conscientious as I am. I don't turn drunks out onto the streets! I use friendly persuasion to get their keys from them. I call cabs for them. I care about innocent families driving home from wherever it was. I do. I promise you that."

"What good does that kind of promise do? You still can't control what happens when they leave your place. I can't accept your kind of work."

"You haven't even tried. You heard what kind of business I'm in, turned your back, and walked away from me. Give a little, Mary. Don't be so hidebound in your dislike of booze. Face the fact that it's here to stay. Learn to deal with it."

"I deal with it on a daily basis," she reminded him hotly. "I know I can't close all the bars in the city, and I'm not trying to, but I don't have to like them—or the people who run them."

He tilted her face up, forcing her to meet his gaze. "But do you like me?" he said. *You loved me, you just never told me so.*

"I did like you." *I love you, but I'll learn not to.*

"I haven't changed. I'm still the same guy you met a few weeks ago, the guy who gave you a ride to work, the guy you had dinner with a couple of times. The guy you laughed with, talked with, the guy who came to help you when you needed it." He closed his eyes for an instant and swallowed visibly. "The guy you made love to as if you were starving for his touch," he added in a low, ragged voice, his gaze hot on her face. "I can't forget that, Mary. I can't forget the way you felt in my arms, the way you moved against me, the way you held me, the way you tasted." He touched her then, sliding the palm of one warm hand around the nape of her neck, and she felt the tremor in his fingers. "Can you forget all that?"

Her heart leapt wildly inside her chest, and she couldn't meet his eyes. "I . . . I will," she said. "I have to. It wouldn't work, Bruce."

"What wouldn't work?"

"Us."

"As lovers? Then what about friends?" Dammit, he was not going to let her go out of his life!

Of course he could sense the need in her, the ache, the yearning for him as a lover as well as a friend. His grip tightened, and he tugged her gently toward him so that her head rested on his shoulder for just an instant before she pulled back, afraid to get caught up in the sensuous pleasure of breathing in his scent. She teetered there on the stair above the landing and then put up her hands, curling them over his shoulders, holding him away from her.

"Bruce, don't." Her voice shook.

"Mary, please. Friends. At least give me that. I need that from you. I want your love, but if you can't give it to me, I'll take whatever you can offer."

She felt his breath on her cheek, felt his hand clench as it slid down her spine to the small of her back. His free one tilted her face up. His eyes were somber, his mouth a straight line. "Please?"

She shivered as his thighs brushed hers, and there was so little strength in her to move away, turn and flee, or even retreat up another stair. "It doesn't feel as if you're asking for just friendship," she said tremulously.

He sighed, frowning, and then said in a resigned tone, "I'm not. I'd like to be able to lie and say that was all I wanted, so maybe you'd give me a chance to get under your defenses, but you'd know I was lying. So I'm telling you the truth. I want more than friendship with you. I want you. I want to take you to bed again and make love to you all night, every night for

. . ." He frowned. "For a lot of nights. I'd give almost anything to have things right between us again. But . . ."

"But not give up your bar."

He looked bleak. "That's right. Because your objection to it is irrational."

"It's not just what you do for a living that tells me you and I could never make it together. We're too different. You like parties. I hate them. You like lots of people around all the time. I like my privacy. You have a big, loving family who may be mad at you right now, or disappointed, or whatever it is they're feeling toward you, but they'll come around and you'll be back in their bosom again, maybe even go home to live. I get along quite well all by myself. No—"

She lifted a hand to stop him from speaking, seeing the flare of compassion in his eyes. What was he going to do, offer to share his big, loving family with her? Until when? Until she changed the rules in the middle of the game and decided she wanted to marry him, make babies with him? She wanted that now, but she knew she couldn't have it. Not with him. Not under the circumstances. He'd said he was in love with her, not that he wanted forever with her. And even if he did want forever, she didn't want that with him. Not now.

"I have to go," she said. "I can't talk anymore."

He stepped aside at last and let her slip by, following her out into the sunny afternoon. He blinked against the brightness.

"Mary."

She squinted up at him, then pulled her sunglasses out of her purse and slipped them on. "Yes?"

"You loved him—Kevin—very much."

It was no question, but she treated it as such. "Yes, I did."

"Do you think you could ever love another man as much?"

"I don't know. Not the same, maybe, but differently. Maybe." *Maybe? Oh, Lord, what an under-statement!*

He leaned one shoulder on the trunk of a cedar tree and looked at her closely. The shadows of fluttering fronds danced over his face and neck, obscuring his expression. "Me?"

"Bruce, please don't," she whispered through the tightness in her throat. "There's no future in it. I know that."

"Well, I don't know it!" he said, his temper flaring again. "Don't I have any say in what happens between us?"

She shook her head, watching the sun and shadows play across his face. "I'm afraid not."

He reached out to her, snatching her sunglasses off, catching her arms in his hands. His grip was hot and hard and almost painfully tight. "And that's it, isn't it, Mary? That's the word you should have been using all along." He searched her eyes. "You're afraid, and you're using my job as an excuse."

She met his heated gaze for a long moment before answering in a rough voice. "Yes," she said. "Yes, I'm afraid. Loving doesn't come easy to me. I loved my parents; they died. I loved my grandparents; they died. And I loved my husband and son. But for all that, for all the fear, I'd take the risk of loving . . . someone else, if I thought it would work. Love is worth a lot of risk and pain. But us?" She shook her head. "That wouldn't work." She stiffened her back, turned it to him, and walked away. When he put a hand on her shoulder, spoke her name harshly, she shrugged free of him, and whirled to face him. "Please leave me alone. I have a life to live. And a bus to catch."

"Right," he said. "Fine. Spend the rest of your life riding buses, Mary, because you're afraid to drive a car. And the rest of your life running away from what *is*, because reality might cause you a little more pain in addition to the kind of joy most people know only in their dreams. But you don't know the meaning of real pain, lady! I'll tell you what real pain is: It's loving a woman for the first time in your life and having to accept the fact that she's going to deny you everything you want simply because she's too much of a coward to reach out and take what's there for her! So good-bye, and good luck, and I hope you catch every bus you ever run for, because I won't be around to take you places anymore."

Nine

"What a juvenile threat to make!" Mary muttered to herself as she strode to the bus stop. "As if I care whether he'll be around with his big, dumb motor-cycle anymore! He sounded about as mature as a high school kid!" She didn't even get to see the rear end of the bus disappearing around the corner or catch a whiff of diesel. She was far too late for that. With a sigh she resigned herself for at least a ten-minute wait, and steeled herself when she heard the roar of a motorcycle from far down the street. If it was Bruce, he turned a corner before he got to where she stood, and she told herself she was glad.

He came to her door twice during the next week, but she saw him through the peephole and refused to answer. He must have seen her shadow darken the tiny viewport, because he fixed his eyes on it, on her unseen face, shrugged, and offered a crooked grin the first time, then nothing more than a shrug the second. Each time he appeared, she stood there long after he'd gone, shaking, asking herself why she hadn't let him in, and then telling herself that there were a thousand valid reasons to keep the man out of her life.

After a third abortive trip to her door he stopped coming. She refused to admit that she missed him. She refused to acknowledge the ache deep inside her when she lay and stared at the ceiling for half the night, an ache that remained when she woke up each morning and that she carried with her to work and school and the library and home again. And then, during a time of near inertia brought on by the start of her now unwanted vacation, it grew, and the loneliness grew, as the days ticked slowly, slowly by.

She was almost relieved when the doorbell rang one morning as she sat at her desk reading—or pretending to herself that she was reading. Anything to break the monotony, even if it was just another tiny glimpse of Bruce, seen through the distorting lens of the peephole.

She looked out the peephole and saw Mr. Taylor standing there, and felt a wave of sick disappointment wash over her. "Hello," she said, opening the door. "What can I do for you?"

"I wondered if you were all right," he said. "I haven't seen you going out to work the last week or so. Wondered if you were sick."

She'd had no idea he kept such close tabs on his tenants. It surprised her. "I'm fine. Thank you. I'm on vacation. It was nice of you to concern yourself, Mr. Taylor." Why hadn't he simply telephoned her? It surely would have been easier than dragging himself away from his television.

"Oh, no trouble," he said, and then stepped aside as Stud came striding around the corner of the hall, gave him a smile and a half-salute, and walked right on in past him.

"Now, just a min—" Mary started to say, but the super reached out, took the door from her hand, and closed it firmly, with himself on the outside and her—along with a stony-faced Stud—on the inside.

"Sorry, but that was the only way I could get in. We are going to talk," he said, leaning against the door.

"No." She glared at him, her chin high, her eyes ablaze. Now that he was there, she could remember all too clearly why she didn't want him in her life on any terms at all. His sex appeal was simply too potent. She loved him too much, wanted him too much. But he was never going to change. And neither was she.

"Yes." His stare from his hazel-green eyes was flat. "If you're on vacation, why aren't you away somewhere?"

"I have no—" What was she supposed to say? *I have no place to go?* She wouldn't admit that to him. "I have no desire to go anywhere."

"Good." The satisfaction in his voice infuriated her for reasons she couldn't begin to understand. She didn't even try. She did, however, try to walk away. If he wanted to stand there propping up her door, she didn't have to watch him do it. She had other things to do. But her attempt was an exercise in futility. One of his hands snaked out and captured her wrist. He didn't hold her tightly, just inescapably, keeping her directly in front of him.

"Good?" she demanded as if she had never intended to do anything but stand there and argue with him. "What's so good about my spending my vacation at home? And what business is it of yours, anyway?"

"At least I don't have to worry about your going to some singles' sex spa!"

"Singles' sex spa?" She gaped at him. "I didn't know such things existed. Name one. Several! I still have two weeks left. Maybe it's not too late to book." What kind of life did he think she led? Singles' sex spas? Good heavens!

He loosened his grip on her wrist, sliding his hand down to link fingers with her. She tried to tug free, to no avail. Either he was stronger than she'd thought, or she was weaker. Her heart hammered high in her throat, nearly choking her. He smelled so good.

"I'm glad you'll be out of that hell hole downtown for a while," he said. "I worry about your being there, Mary. Have you decided if you're going back when your contract's up?"

She had decided. Negatively. "I don't see what concern that is of yours."

"It matters to me where you work."

"Bruce!" Her temper flared. "How can you say that? I mean, after—" She broke off with an angry splutter.

"After I told you that my work was none of your business, that I wouldn't change jobs to suit you because you were being irrational?"

She nodded vehemently and managed to surprise him by snatching her hand out of his clasp. She paced away from him. "Your memory is fine," she said, turning to face him from a safer distance. "That's exactly what I meant."

"Well, your job is dangerous and dirty, and it makes you unhappy."

"Talk about irrational! Dangerous and dirty and miserable as it might be, what I do is one hell of a lot more important to the quality of community life than what you do!"

His eyes darkened as he followed her into the living room. "Is it? Is it really? How many of those people you dry out and counsel want to be dried out and counseled? Or are they there because they've been dragged in kicking and screaming off the street, and the only alternative is jail?"

"Is this what you came here for, Bruce? To harangue me about my work? I don't want to hear it any more than you want to hear my opinion of your job. So we have nothing to discuss. And even if we did, it seems we couldn't do it in a rational manner.

I have better ways to spend my time than arguing with you."

"Yes, we do have things to discuss! We are going to talk about my bar and your reasons for disliking it."

"My reasons are mine, and I feel they are valid. And it isn't just your bar I hate!"

"Isn't it? What I think is that—"

"What you think simply doesn't concern me. Your pouring booze down people's throats does, and—"

"The people who come to the Raven's Nest come because they want to be there," he interrupted, overriding her completely. "I don't force anyone. They're looking for a few relaxing hours, some companionship, some pleasure after a hard day at work."

"I say your customers are there because they're looking to get bombed out of their minds in order to forget the day's trials!" she shouted. "The only thing that makes it look marginally better than what my customers do is that yours do it from glasses in a dingy little room with tables and chairs instead of in a back alley or on a bench in Pigeon Park with their bottles in brown paper bags!"

Bruce came to a halt not a foot from her, arms folded across his chest. He was breathing hard, his eyes flaming with annoyance. Uncrossing his arms, he clenched his fists at his sides. "Oh, come on, Mary!" he said disgustedly. "When's the last time you were in a neighborhood pub?"

She planted her hands on her hips. "A little more than four years ago," she enunciated clearly, pointedly.

He raised his brows. "Looking for sympathy? Want me to lay off because you're a poor, bereaved widow whose husband was killed by a boozer?"

She gasped. "Of course not!" But she wondered, sickly, for just a moment, if his suggestion was so very far off the mark. She rejected the idea at once. Her objection to bars stemmed from more than the fact that a drunk had killed her husband and child. It went deeper than that, was far more basic. It wasn't just a personal vendetta. Yet . . . why hadn't it manifested itself before that terrible time four years ago?

"And did you see any drunks?" he went on, looming over her.

She tilted back her head in order to see him. "How would I know? You can't look at any given person and say, 'That's a drunk,' unless he's falling off his chair or acting the fool or lying in the doorway in a pool of—*You,* as experienced as you might be, can't tell just by looking at him if the person you're serving can handle what you're selling him. There are people who are truly allergic to booze. Trouble is, most of them don't know it, or if they do, won't admit it. But one drink, or maybe two, and their judgment is shot, so they can't tell if they're drunk or not. And those are the ones who concern me. The ones you can't pick out of a crowd. The ones you won't refuse to serve because you have no way of knowing you should!"

"I've already told you, I don't serve people who have obviously had too much."

"What about those who have obviously had just enough?"

He frowned, linked his hands together behind his back, and walked away from her, turning at the far side of the room and leaning on the mantel. "All right. I admit there's a fine line that maybe I cross sometimes. Inadvertently. Unknowingly. But people have to learn to look after themselves. People should take responsibility for their own actions."

Mary walked to where he stood and spoke earnestly. "That's what you've got to understand, Bruce. Drunks can't. For the simple reason that once drunk, they become totally irresponsible, and you can't make them see sense no matter how hard you try. It's like trying to reason with a two-year-old. You can't do it, because two-years-olds aren't reasonable people yet, and when a person's drunk, he's lost his ability to reason. So the thing to do is not let them get drunk in the first place, and the way to do that is to not serve them alcohol."

"That's not reasonable," he said, putting his hands on her arms. "You can take a drink or two without going overboard. So can I. So can most people. So should we stop serving the majority because a very small minority is unable for one reason or another to handle themselves with a bit of alcohol in their blood?"

"How do you know I can take a drink or two without going overboard?" she demanded, shrugging him off. "You've never seen me take a drink. And you won't. So if you've come here to preach to me about how a little social drink never hurt anybody, you're in the wrong place, buddy. I do not drink."

"That's fine with me," he said, suddenly sounding tired and dispirited. "I never try to force alcohol on anyone. And like I said, I didn't come here to argue with you. I came to tell you about the Raven's Nest and to ask if you would come and see it, just once. So you'd know what kind of establishment Jake and I run. Mary, please. I want you to know what it's like before you throw away what you and I can have."

"Bruce . . . don't." *Don't be nice, don't be reasonable, don't remind me of what we had together.* Her throat hurt. Her knees felt weak. She managed to get to the couch, where she sank down, her hands linked tightly in her lap. "I don't go to bars."

"Come to mine," he said in a soft, urgent tone, crouching before her. "See what it's like. That's all I ask. Just give it a try."

"What's to try? I don't drink."

"That doesn't matter. Probably one person in four, maybe even one in two or three doesn't drink there either."

"No?" She raised a skeptical brow. "So what's the point in going to a bar?"

"To socialize. To be with friends. We serve free virgin drinks to anyone who comes and tells us he or she is the designated driver of the evening."

She was taken aback. That didn't sound very profitable. How could a person stay in business giving drinks away? "Free?" she asked suspiciously, as he rose to sit near her.

"Absolutely free. No questions asked."

"I . . . That's nice." Suddenly she realized that they were sitting in her living room holding a fairly civilized conversation. It gave her a surprisingly warm feeling, one almost of hope. They weren't arguing any longer. Did that mean they might become friends again? More than friends? If they both set their minds to it?

"Most reputable places do that now, Mary."

"I didn't know that."

He smiled gently. "Probably because you don't go to bars."

"I used to," she said musingly. "Kevin and I—" She broke off, lowering her head, biting her lip.

"It's okay to mention Kevin," he said. "I know he was part of your life. It would be odd if you didn't talk about him sometimes. And when you went to bars with Kevin, did you take a drink or two?"

"Yes." She looked over at him. "Bruce, the day . . . the day of the accident I'd had a bottle of cider at the beach. We'd gone for a picnic. I've always wondered if I hadn't had it, would my reflexes have been that much better? Maybe I'd have seen the pickup come through the stop sign. Maybe I could have slowed down, or speeded up, or swerved. Got out of the way somehow and . . ."

He reached out to touch her, then pulled his hand back. Not now. Not yet. If he touched her, he'd lose his ability to talk rationally. As it was, he was holding on to it only by the finest margin. To be this near her, to breathe in her natural perfume, to see the pain in her eyes and not hold her was torture. "You've been beating yourself with that for a long time, haven't you?" he asked gruffly. "Mary, one bottle of cider with food did not hamper your reflexes. The accident was not your fault."

She breathed out a long sigh and nodded. "I know that. My mind knows that. But some small part of me questions it now and again, asks 'what if.' What if I'm one of that small percentage who is truly allergic to alcohol, just the way someone like you is allergic to pollen?"

He was silent again for a few minutes. "I don't know, Mary. Maybe you are, but I doubt it seriously. And do you think we should run around cutting down all flowering trees and shrubs, digging up every garden in the city, just because I might have a sneezing fit while driving and run my car into someone else?"

She shook her head. "Of course not. But look at it this way, too, Bruce. Now that I know you're hyper-allergic to flowers, I'll never throw a daisy in your face again."

He grinned wryly. "Thank you for that, if nothing else." To her surprise he got to his feet. Stuffing his hands in his pockets, he said, "I've never looked on alcoholism as a possible allergy to alcohol. And you're right, I have no way of knowing which of my customers might be afflicted. I'll get out of your hair now. I can see you were studying, and I have to get to work. But think about what I've said, Mary. Please, just think about coming by and checking the place out."

The look she gave him was obdurate. She shook her head. "No, Bruce. I'm sorry, but no."

He looked at her for a few moments longer, then turned on his heel and went out the door, closing it quietly behind him.

•   •   •

"Aggie, are you free this afternoon?" She didn't expect her friend to be available on a Friday afternoon, but it was certainly worth a try.

"Not exactly, Mary, but if it's important, I could be." Aggie's voice sounded tinny, so Mary knew she was using her little cordless phone, probably somewhere outside in the garden. "It's just a meeting of the pollution control committee, and then Steve and I have plans for the evening. But the committee could do without me for once. Carol from next door could read my report on disposable diapers. Why don't you join Steve and me? We're going to Bart and Nancy's to help christen their new pool. They'd love to have you."

"No, no. Thanks anyway. I'll pass."

"You sound pretty far down. What's up, pal? You know if you need me, I'm here. How's your escort service stud?"

"Uh . . . he's not with an escort service after all."

"That's great."

"Well, no, and that's why I'm calling. Aggie, would you say I'm 'hidebound' in the way I've come to feel about drinking?"

"Well, that might be a bit of a strong term. If you were really fanatical, you'd never come here, since both Steve and I take a drink now and then. And for that matter, until four years ago, so did you."

"I know. But since then. Have I become too harsh a critic of people who do drink?"

"Critical maybe. But you're never rabid, so don't worry about it, unless . . . Hey, I'm getting the feeling you're not telling me what the real problem is, and I figure it has to do with your stud. If he doesn't work for or own an escort service, what does he do that's got your shirt tied around your neck?"

Mary let out a slow breath. "He runs a bar."

There was dead silence on the other end of the line, then a muffled sound, and Mary asked indignantly, "Agnes, are you laughing?"

"Whoops! When you call me that, I know I'm in trouble. Sorry, Mare. But I can't help it. It seems almost like . . . well . . . poetic justice, I guess."

"Why poetic justice?" asked Mary huffily.

"Well, I mean, you and a bartender? After all these years of your being so militantly against drinking in any form?"

"Aggie! I have not been militant! You just said that 'hidebound' was too strong a word, that I've never been rabid, and now you're calling me militant?"

"I was trying to be tactful, you ninny. You have so been militant! In fact, there have been times when I've had to forcibly restrain Steve to keep him from buying you a little axe."

"Axe?"

"Carry Nation."

"Oh. Bruce called me that," Mary said in a small voice. "Aggie, I didn't mean to be militant. Am I a real pain in the butt about it?"

"Only sometimes, hon. And we love you. We understand why you feel that way. We can accept it. It would just make life a little easier if you'd accept that we like to take the odd drink when we sit and relax."

"I thought I did."

"You just have this way of looking warily and suspiciously at anyone who's sipping a glass of wine or a can of beer, as if you expect us to grow long talons and hair on the backs of our hands."

"I'm sorry. I didn't mean to."

"That's okay. Like I said, we love you and understand. Now what was it you wanted me to do this afternoon? That committee meeting is beginning to sound less and less interesting."

"No. It's okay. You go and give your report. What I wanted was just what I got. To talk. Thanks, Aggie. I love you too. 'Bye, now."

"Wait—" Aggie started, but Mary quickly hung up and didn't answer the phone when it rang almost at

once. If she was going to do it, she'd just go ahead
and do it. She didn't need Aggie to hold her hand.
Heavens, anyone could walk into a neighborhood
pub and order a drink! A companion was completely
unnecessary.

Still, it took her until nearly eight that evening to
gather up the courage to do it. She dressed carefully, not too flashy, not too tame, in a dark blue
suede skirt that came just below midthigh, a pale
blue angora sweater with a wide red patent leather
belt, and matching red heels to make her legs look
great. She fastened her hair back loosely with a flat
red satin bow at her nape, letting the curls cascade
down between her shoulder blades. If she was going
to surprise Bruce, she wanted to do it right.

It was a noisy place, full of what she knew Bruce
liked: laughter, music, and people. Mary wrinkled
her nose as she walked through the door. There was
smoke in the air, hanging like a blue cloud near the
ceiling, the ventilation fans unable to cope with it
adequately, but that was the only point she could
have made against the Raven's Nest. A group of
people at a nearby table were singing something
about the best baseball team in the world, arms
linked, swaying as they sang. A few others threw
darts at a board. More stood hollering and ribbing
each other at video games in one corner. Someone
swooped past her carrying a tray filled with beer
glasses, never spilling a drop. There were two men
behind the bar, neither of whom was Bruce. Up a
flight of three steps were several empty tables crowded
under a massive television screen, which at the moment was blank.

Carefully Mary made her way to one of the vacant
tables, sat down, and looked around, pleasantly surprised by what she saw. The decor was nice, with
light green drapes in the latest fashion to match the

upholstery of the booths that lined two walls. It was a friendly place, with stark line drawings on the walls depicting scenes from old logging days. In one corner stood a bare, sparsely branched tree with a pile of twigs and sticks in its limbs. Of course, she thought, a raven's nest, or what some decorator had made up to look like one.

The table where she sat alone was roomy, with three more comfortable chairs. This was not a crowded, dingy place full of furtive drinkers. Of course it wasn't. She chided herself for having half-expected it to be. She'd been in pubs before. She knew what they were like. Had she, with her adamant hatred of any and all such establishments, allowed her mind to warp her memory? It seemed so. This was just a nice, normal bar, filled with nice, normal people, having a few drinks in a nice, normal way. Nothing terrible. Nothing threatening. She leaned forward and rested her elbows on the table, chin on her hands, trying desperately to relax and look as though she belonged.

Shoving aside the clean ashtray, Mary picked up the folded menu from the center of the table and glanced at it, amazed at the variety of food available along with the peanuts and potato chips and cheese snacks.

"You all alone?" asked a man from behind her. She turned, looking up. A tall, bearded man stood there, smiling down at her through the dark bush surrounding his mouth. "Want to join us?" He indicated a table where three other men and two women sat. One of the women gave her a smile and a wave, obviously offering a welcome.

"I . . . uh, no, thanks. I'm . . . waiting for someone. But it was nice of you to ask."

"Sure, no prob'. Change your mind, come on over. I'm Chuck."

"Okay. Thanks, Chuck."

The waiter swooped by again with another tray of

beer and set glasses quickly around Chuck's table. Then, holding his money folded in between his fingers, he came to Mary. "Hi there. What can I get for you?"

"Uh . . . a glass of dry white wine, please."

"Sure. One house white coming up. Saw you looking at the menu. You hungry?"

Mary shook her head. "Is Bruce Hagendorn here tonight?"

The waiter looked mystified. "Bruce . . . Oh! Stud? He was. He should be. Must be in the back with Jake. You know him? Want to see him?"

"Not if he's busy. I can wait."

Her wine came, and she drank it in tiny sips. It tasted better than she'd remembered, tangy and crisp and slightly tingly on her tongue, icy cold and pleasant in her throat, yet warm in her stomach. As she sipped she people-watched, enjoying trying to decide who did what.

"How you doin'?" asked the waiter. "Can I get you a refill?"

Mary looked at her glass in astonishment. It was empty. She hesitated only briefly. "No, thanks, but some mineral water with a twist would be great."

"You didn't like that wine? There are others," the young man said.

"No, no. It was nice wine." And it had been. But Mary reminded herself that after so long without any alcohol in her system, she'd be wise to take it easy. "Just the mineral water, thanks."

She continued to gaze around, and presently the waiter returned. "I saw Stud and told him someone was out here waiting for him. He says he'll be out in a bit. Can I tell him your name?"

Mary felt a mischievous grin spread across her face. "No," she said, and laughed softly. "I'll just surprise him. Tell him not to hurry," she added, although she felt increasingly conspicuous being all alone. It would be worth it to surprise Bruce.

"Okay. I'll pass on the message."

Half an hour later, she was tired of sitting there pretending she was having a good time. When the waiter made another pass near her table, she caught his arm as he was about to move away. "Listen, do you know those people over there?" She indicated the table where the bearded man sat with his friends, laughing at some joke.

"Sure. Why?" The waiter frowned. "They're not giving you a hard time, are they? Normally they're really nice folks. Regulars here. The guy with the beard is a teacher. I think the others are too."

"Oh, no. They were very nice. Asked me to join them. I just wondered if . . ."

"That'd be fine," the young man assured her. "You go ahead and join them if you want. I'll carry your drink over, okay? Stud and Jake are in some kind of deep conference. No telling how long they'll be."

The strangers didn't remain that way for long, and conversation was quick, sprightly, interesting. Mary realized after twenty minutes that she was having more fun than she'd had in a long time. She felt at home with these people, and even though they were all drinking beer, they were simply sipping, the beverage was just something to keep their throats damp as they discussed everything from class size to glasnost.

When her red satin bow began to slide down the back of her hair, Chuck deftly reclipped it, saying that as an elementary school teacher he did that about twenty times a day. "Little girls and their pretty ribbons," he said, shaking his head while he fiddled with her hair.

"You call Mary a little girl?" asked one of the other men, lifting his brows. "If that's what you think, change chairs with me. I think she looks all grown-up." He grinned lasciviously but without malice, and Mary laughed at them both.

Chuck spread her hair out over her back and patted her shoulder affectionately. "We'll wait a bit and see if Mary's date shows up, and then we'll decide who sits in what chair." He placed a big fist on the table in mock threat that his friend took about as seriously as Mary did.

The waiter came back and brought Mary a refill, though she hadn't asked. "Stud said to buy you one of whatever you were drinking, and tell you he'd be finished in five minutes."

She felt a little thrill of excitement go through her at the thought of what he'd say when he saw her. He'd be pleased, that much she knew. The butterflies increased in her stomach. Would he know why she was there? Would he be able to read between the lines of her action, and realize that she was in effect telling him of the depths of her feelings for him? Because she wouldn't be here if she didn't love him. She knew that now. She only hoped he'd know it too.

It was closer to fifteen minutes before he came, though, and Mary was on her way back from the restroom with one of the other women at the table when she spotted Bruce standing under the television screen looking around, a perplexed expression on his face. She laughed and slipped her arm out of June's light clasp. "Bruce!" she called. "Over here."

The look on his face was priceless, Mary thought, collapsing into her chair in gales of laughter. "Bruce, oh, Bruce, you look so funny! I surprised you, didn't I?"

"You surprised me, all right," he said gruffly, lifting her bodily out of her chair, tucking her firmly against his side. "What in the hell are you doing in here?" He glanced around at the new friends she had made. "Do you know these people?"

"I do now," she said, and made quick introductions during which, oddly, Bruce showed little interest, considering his liking for parties and people. "They saw I was alone and asked me to join them."

"I don't believe this," said Bruce. "I'm not just surprised, I'm damn well astounded! Come on. I'm taking you home."

Mary stared up at him, still laughing. "Why, Bruce! Aren't you being a little heavy-handed? I'm enjoying myself here. I like your bar."

"Of course you do," he said. "You'd enjoy anything right now! You're popped right out of your mind!"

"I'm *what*?" she said, her mouth falling open. "I'll have you know I only had—"

"Save it," he said with a grunt, picking her up and draping her over his shoulder as he strode down the steps to the main part of the room. He spoke briefly to someone, and then they were crossing through a kitchen, out of the pub and into the cool night air.

"Now suppose you tell me exactly what is bugging you?" she demanded as he set her on her feet, one hand still square in the middle of her back, holding a fistful of hair as if he were afraid she'd try to escape back inside. "I just wanted to surprise you. I thought you'd be glad."

"I'm surprised all right," he said, dumping her into the front seat of his car. "As to glad, that remains to be seen. Depends on what you feel about tonight, tomorrow."

"What does that mean?" she asked, struggling with her seat belt. He slid behind the wheel and took over the task from her.

"It means that I don't mind if you get mildly potted now and then. I'd rather you didn't, but if you do, it's no major crime. However, you might not be so happy in the morning."

"I'll be just fine in the morning," she said indignantly. "And what do you mean, mildly potted? I am nothing of the sort! I had one glass of wine and—"

"It's the 'and' that'll do it every time," he said succinctly. "Tom said there was a lady waiting to see me. Then, a bit later, he said the lady wouldn't give him her name. Shortly after that he said there was no point in my hurrying because the lady had already been picked up by a schoolteacher with a beard and six hands."

"A schoolteacher, yes, and a beard, certainly, but he only had two hands that I saw, and he kept both of them above the table the whole time! And it was that same waiter who told me it was perfectly safe for me to join Chuck and his friends!"

"Mary, for the love of mike, why didn't you give the waiter your name? Why did you sit out there and drink, waiting for me? You know I'd have been out there like a shot if I'd known it was you. Especially if I'd known you were drinking," he added almost to himself.

It dawned on her that he truly did believe she was drunk. For a moment she tried to be furious, but the ridiculous side of the situation appealed to her, and she bubbled inside with mischief. He thought she was drunk, did he? All right then, she'd give him drunk.

"Who did you think it was?" she cooed, sliding her hand from his knee to very high up his thigh.

"I don't know." His words came too quickly, his voice ragged. "Some groupie or other."

It pleased her that he hadn't hurried out to see a groupie. "There are lots of those, aren't there?"

He cleared his throat and shrugged. "Some. I don't encourage them, you know." He took her hand off his thigh. He wasn't encouraging her, either.

"Why not? Isn't it good for the ego?" She put her hand back on his leg.

"My ego doesn't need that. Why don't you close your eyes and rest until we get home?" He sounded desperate.

"Because I'm not tired," she said, her fingers busy again. "And I'm not drunk either, Bruce."

He stilled her hand, pinning it with his own. "Sure, sweetheart. I know."

"I did enjoy myself tonight, Bruce. And I do like your bar."

"That's great," he said sourly.

"Well, you don't have to sound so grouchy about it. You invited me, remember?"

"Yes, I did, didn't I?"

"Bruce? Are you mad at me?" She undid her seat belt and slid close to him, putting her head on his shoulder.

"No, I am not, but I will be if you don't get back over there where you belong and get that belt done up again."

"But I want to be close to you." She managed a faint, fairly authentic little hiccup.

"Oh, hell!" He eased the car into the curb and fumbled around until he found the center belt, snapped it across her lap, and pulled back out into traffic, one arm around her. "I want to be close to you, too, but I didn't want it to be like this, love." His voice seemed thick.

"I like it when you call me that," she said. "It makes me feel all warm and tingly inside, as if we're about to make love. That's the way I planned for this evening to end, you know. With us making love together. I've been looking forward to it."

He laughed without humor. "Me, too, but not tonight."

She nestled next to him and closed her eyes, pretending to herself that she was in the condition he thought she was, wondering if that was the way a drunk woman would act, even one who was only "mildly potted" as he'd put it. Presently he nudged her and said that they were home. Keeping her body soft and relaxed, she let him take her out of the car.

"Give me your key," he said outside her door, and Mary pretended to search, carefully avoiding the little zipper pocket where she'd tucked it. She had no intention of sleeping in her own apartment tonight, though she hadn't expected to have to fake a key loss to make it happen. After a good search, she shrugged. "I guess you'll have to take me home with you."

Quickly Bruce emptied her purse all over the floor and sorted through the contents while Mary stood there, laughing at him. "Give up," she said. "It's not there. Of course we could always go and get a spare from Mr. Taylor."

He looked at her laughing face in exasperation, his lips twitching. "All right," he said. "Come on." He tugged her toward the stairs.

He unlocked his door and closed it quickly behind him, leaning on it, looking at her with a bemused expression. "Mary, I never thought I'd see you like this."

No, she thought, he probably hadn't, and it was time she convinced him of the truth. "You're not seeing me any different than I've ever been. No—" She paused, unclipped her red bow and shook her hair free. "That's not quite true. You're seeing me as I should be, open, relaxed with you, free to tell you the way I feel." She stroked the red satin over his jaw, down his neck. "I love you, Bruce. And I want to spend the night with you."

"Sweetheart , . . don't." He caught her hand, held it down by her side. "Please, don't do this, don't say things like that tonight."

"I have to. Now that I've got my courage up, I have to tell you how I feel. I love you, and I want you, and nothing else matters."

"Dammit, did you ever hear the term 'Dutch courage'?"

"Of course I've heard the term, but how often do I have to tell you, I'm not drunk! Bruce, I was drinking—"

He stopped her words with his fingers over her lips. "Maybe not drunk the way we usually mean by the term, but your inhibitions sure have taken a beating," he said, taking her to the couch and seating her.

"Now, you stay put," he said, tenderly running a hand over her hair, brushing it back from her face. "I'm going to make you some coffee. And then . . ."

"And then?" she asked hopefully, her eyes dancing. It was past time, she thought, to tell him she'd been drinking mineral water since that single glass of wine, but she'd wait until he thought he'd sobered her up with coffee. Then she planned to seduce him very, very slowly and extremely thoroughly. When she got through with him, he'd know he'd been seduced.

He laughed quietly. "Sweetheart, I promise you, if you still feel the same way tomorrow, we'll make love so many times, you'll drown me in my own wading pool just to get rid of me."

Wading pool. She sat there smiling as he left to make coffee, remembering the day she had seen a hunk in a wading pool and pitched a vase of flowers at him. Little had she known that in only a month or so, she was going to be head over heels in love with that same hunk, aching with wanting him, and having him refuse her because he thought she was drunk. She laughed again. Maybe it was too soon to convince him of the truth. Maybe she could have a little more fun with this entire situation. And what better way to seduce the man than the way he'd unwittingly seduced her on that very first day?

She got to her feet. Quietly she walked to the balcony door, slid it open without a sound, stepped outside, and stood breathing in the sweet night air. She noticed that the stars, hardly ever visible there in the city, seemed a little brighter. There was that crazy pool belonging to that crazy man who was still making coffee, and presumably a big mess, in the kitchen, oblivious of her.

He would not, she vowed, remain oblivious much longer. Mary felt a joyous laugh bubbling up in her chest and gave it free rein as she whipped her sweater off over her head, kicked off her shoes, unbuckled her belt, unzipped her skirt, and peeled it down with her panty hose, draping everything over the rail. She shed her bra, then stepped into the water. It felt nice up over her ankles. Gingerly she sat down, stretched her legs out over the side, and leaned back against the slide, hands behind her head, as he had done that first time she saw him. Oh! It was heavenly.

With one hand she sloshed water over herself, feeling her nipples pucker in the cool air. She laughed, tilted her face to the sky, and sang, "San-ta Lucia, Santa . . . Lucia!"

Ten

Behind her the door was rolled farther open noisily, rapidly, and Bruce came out, stopping to stare at her in horrified fascination. "Mary! For pete's sake! What are you doing?" he asked in a hoarse whisper.

In a normal conversational tone she replied, "Trying out your wading pool. After all, we uninhibited people do lots of things like this. Care to join me?"

Crouching, he slid his arms under her and lifted her out. "Oh, Lordy, Lordy," he said, groaning. "What am I going to do with you, woman?"

"Make love to me," she said, smiling happily up at him. "That's all, Bruce. Just make love to me."

He stood her in the bathroom and wrapped her in an inadequate towel, drying her legs and arms briskly with another. "That's all, huh? Just make love to you."

"That's all," she assured him, snaking her arms around his neck and moving against him.

He took her arms down from around his neck, pushing her away. "No."

"I can walk a straight line," she said, and dropped her towel, walking away from him, straight—very straight—into his bedroom. He followed. "I can stand on one foot and touch my finger to my nose." She stood on one foot, touched her finger to her nose, and fell sideways onto his bed, to lie there, laughing up at him, arms out to him. "Come here, Stud," she whispered seductively. "Come and love me."

He sat down on the foot of the bed, lolled back, and flung his arm up over his head, roaring with laughter.

"What is so funny?" she demanded, getting up on her knees and glaring at him. This was not the way it was supposed to work, dammit! He was supposed to be completely at her mercy by now.

He captured her and hauled her down onto his chest. "You are, love. My love. My funny, funny love! You are so funny, I don't think I could make love to you now to save my life. I'd only want to laugh at your antics."

He rolled her onto her back, then got to his feet. Opening a drawer in his bureau, he dug out a big T-shirt and sat her up, tugging it over her head, putting her arms into the sleeves. Then, pulling the covers from under her, he straightened her on the mattress and covered her right up to her chin. "Good night," he said firmly.

Her mouth trembled. Some fine seductress she'd turned out to be. "Aren't you coming to bed?"

He shook his head. "I'll sleep on the couch."

"Bruce . . . I do love you, you know, and I am sober. I only drank mineral water. Well, and one glass of wine."

He frowned, hesitating. "If you were only drinking mineral water, how come you let a strange school-teacher pick you up?"

She sat up, linked her hands behind his neck, and said, "I remember another day when I was completely sober, maybe not completely sane, mind you, but completely sober, that I let a strange ex-hockey player on a motorcycle pick me up."

He blew out a long breath. "Yeah. Well, that was different."

"Different . . . how?"

He slid closer. "I don't know, but it must have been."

"I guess so, because look where I ended up. Not in some schoolteacher's bed."

His hands moved around her waist. "Mary . . . ?" He wanted so badly to believe she was completely sober, meant everything she was saying, but he couldn't. Not quite.

"Hush, love. Come to bed."

"Are you sure?"

"I'm sure I love you," she said as she nestled closer, her hands beginning a slow, sweet exploration of his back, while her mouth played over his face.

With a groan he stood, shucked most of his clothes, and slid in beside her, drawing her close. He could hold her, just hold her. Maybe she'd fall asleep.

She kissed his throat, moved on down to his chest, her fingers tangling in the mat of hair there, her lips finding one hard little nipple, enclosing it with a kiss, then sucking gently. His breathing quickened. He hardened against her. His arms tightened. She was not falling asleep.

"Stop it," he said harshly, and she laughed throatily, knowing he didn't mean it.

"No," she said, and didn't stop. She traced the shape of his body, down his side, onto his hip, her nail drawing a fine line along his skin until she came to the elastic of his underwear. Then, shyly, almost tentatively, she ran her finger around the elastic line, down the front, and cupped his manhood in her hand through the fine knit fabric.

"Oh, Lord!" he said. "Mary, please . . ."

"Please what?" she asked, stroking him, curling her hand around his flesh, moving it gently. "More? Like that? Teach me, Bruce. Tell me what you like."

"I mean . . . don't." He groaned.

She laughed softly against his chest. "No, you don't."

"I . . . oh, hell, you're right!" he said. He tugged at

the T-shirt he'd put on her, pulling it up over her head.

She inserted her hand within the tight underwear, and he moved sharply as her palm stroked over him. "Ahh!" he sighed, lifting himself, grasping his briefs in one hand and snatching them off entirely. He turned her onto her back, covered her mouth with his, and kissed her deeply. "If you hate me in the morning, Mary, I'll never talk to you again," he said moments later, and she laughed at him, filled with love and tenderness and need.

"I won't hate you, my love. How can I ever hate you when I love you so much. Hurry, Bruce. Please. I can't wait any longer for you."

And this time he did hurry, and she didn't have to wait. But later at dawn he teased her in the clear, golden light until she was nearly incoherent, and then loved her until they both fell into a deep, sated sleep.

"Don't ever leave me," he said, as they stood in the shower together, and she promised she wouldn't. Yet, even as she promised him with words and deeds, the back of her mind kept trying to send urgent messages forward, saying that nothing was resolved between them, that they were in a state of limbo. Somehow she hushed that part of her consciousness, telling herself that she'd think again after Monday night was over, that this time was hers to take, that she was entitled to one weekend of loving. Easily, too easily, the sensuous part of her nature took over. It was good. It was right. She was deeply and irrevocably in love, and she would have this weekend!

"Come home to me," she whispered as he bent over her later, dressed for his night's work. "I'll be waiting."

He smiled and patted the bed at her side where the take-out chicken boxes still lay, evidence of their picnic supper. "Right here?"

"Right here."

• • •

And she was. He slipped in beside her and gathered her close at three o'clock in the morning, and she awoke slowly to his touches, then responded quickly again, her eager body demanding immediate release.

"Not this time," he murmured into her sweet-scented hair. "We have all night, all of tomorrow, and the next day. We'll take it slow, discover a thousand ways to pleasure each other."

"Mmm," she agreed, taking his hand and lifting it to her mouth. "Saturday night—what's left of it." She kissed one of his fingers, drew it into her mouth, and sucked gently for a moment.

"Saturday night will be over before you know it if you don't stop that," he said, his voice a husky grumble that she didn't believe at all.

"Then Sunday," she said, kissing one of his nipples, sucking on it as she had his finger.

He shifted to one side, exposing the rest of his chest to her exploring mouth. "That was for Sunday in the daytime," he said. "How about Sunday night?"

She counted off Sunday night on his other nipple, taking a long time to find it, an even longer time to finish her task.

"And Monday?" he asked moments later, his voice thinner, almost breathless. "What about Monday?"

"Mmm, I'm getting there," she said teasingly, her mouth moving slowly, tantalizingly down his chest, across his rigid abdomen. "Now, let me see. How should we count Monday?"

He took her head in his hands and showed her.

Then, when they were both about to explode, he rolled away from her, flipped her onto her back, clasped her knees in his hands, and moved them up and apart. "I get to count off Monday night," he said, sliding his hands up the insides of her thighs, his eyes intent on her face.

"Yes," she whispered. "Oh, yes," and squeezed her

eyes tightly shut in ecstasy as his hot breath fanned across her lower belly, his silky mustache tickled her thighs, and his mouth claimed her femininity in a devastating kiss of love, and her last coherent thought was that she wanted Monday night never to end.

It did, of course. On Tuesday, although she didn't have to go to work at the center, she still had to put in an appearance at the university. Bruce was still sleeping when she crept from his bed, gathered up her clothing, cast one appalled glance at the crumpled T-shirt that had been all she'd worn since Saturday evening, and rushed into the bathroom to change.

Then, tiptoeing out, she took the stairs to her own apartment where she showered, dressed, and rushed out to catch her bus. Her mind felt numb except for random thoughts that kept intruding—memories of Kevin, of Andy, of a drunk who'd come out of nowhere and ended their lives, and, in effect, hers.

Where had he done his drinking? In a nice place like the Raven's Nest? Maybe even that very place! And she had visited it, added to the profits that kept it going. She was as guilty as the drunk driver had been, and she ached with sorrow for what she had done, not only to the memories she'd tried to preserve and hold intact, inviolate, but to Bruce as well, and her own sense of justice. The thoughts kept coming, blocking concentration, and she sat in a daze of misery, staring at a page she never turned.

When she emerged later that afternoon from the cool atmosphere of the library, the guilt and misery were just as strong, and when she came out of the building on Wednesday afternoon, the sound of the revving motorcycle added to her hurt.

"I thought you'd be at work," she said, shaking her head when Bruce dismounted and tried to put the red helmet on her.

"I called in sick."

She looked at him sharply, then away. "You aren't."

"No. Yes. Heartsick." He touched her face, turning it up to him. "Mary, why did you leave like that yesterday? Without waking me? Without saying good-bye? And why weren't you there waiting for me when I got home from work?"

She lowered her eyes. She couldn't look at him, at the hurt in his face. "Because . . . because it was Tuesday. Our weekend was over. Is over."

"And everything else?"

She nodded, sick with anguish.

He'd known it. She wouldn't have left like that if she'd meant to come back. He didn't know why he'd wanted it confirmed, because he wasn't about to accept it. "No."

"Yes. I'm sorry. I've done a terrible thing. I know that." Her voice, low to begin with, dropped to a whisper. "I shouldn't have made love with you when I knew that there were too many problems we hadn't resolved, problems we can never resolve. Oh, Lord, I'm so ashamed!"

"You love me. And I love you. We deserved our weekend of showing each other how much," he said in a low, taut voice, acutely aware of the group of people waiting for the bus not ten feet away.

"And we deserve a lot more than a weekend to-gether, Mary."

"No. That weekend was wrong. All along I knew I should leave. I should never have gone to the bar, but I'd convinced myself that I—we—could make it work, that love was enough."

"It is!"

"It's not. All weekend my conscience kept telling me to go, but . . ."

"But what? You didn't go, Mary. You stayed. Why?"

"Because you were there holding me, touching me, making love to me. Because I'd been so lonely and wanted you so much. Because I—" No. She wasn't going to say that again. It was true, but what good did it do to keep saying it? It changed nothing. "I stayed, loved you, in spite of what you are, in spite of the way I feel about what you do."

"You're saying I seduced you," he said with desperate, quiet anger, "and we both know it was the other way around."

"Friday it was the other way around. And that's why I'm so ashamed. Oh, Lord, I feel so guilty!"

He clasped her arm and all but dragged her several more feet away from the people in the bus shelter, shoving her into a small alcove in the hedge and onto a wrought iron bench.

"Yet what about Saturday night?" he asked, standing over her, not acknowledging her admission. "I left you for eight hours. I wasn't there seducing you, but you were waiting for me when I got home. You were all alone then, Mary. You can't blame my seduction, or anything but your own needs and desires and love for that one!"

"It was the loneliness," she whispered. "I couldn't stand it any longer."

His face lost color. His dark mustache looked jet black against the white skin around his mouth. "I remember your saying that you were tired of being lonely that first time we went to bed together. Was that the only reason you made love with me, then? Loneliness? You were using me, Mary?"

She didn't deny it, and he felt a rage like none he'd ever felt before—and betrayal and hurt. "I won't be treated that way! When a woman goes to bed with me, she'd better be prepared to admit that it's because she wants me above all other men, not because I'm a substitute for somebody else!"

"Not a sub—"

He interrupted, cutting her off as if she hadn't even tried to speak. "You thought it was all right, didn't you, to use me that way because in your warped judgment, I'm just as responsible for your loneliness as the guy who served the drunk who killed your husband?"

"No! Bruce, no! You're not the one who's guilty! It's me! I'm the one who—"

"Ahh . . . what's the use," he said, jamming the red helmet onto his own head, leaping astride the bike and roaring out of the bus zone just as the big vehicle came around the corner.

The bus came to a breathy halt, and she boarded it, found a seat, and crouched there, head bent, hearing the doors hiss shut, hearing the finality of it all. She squeezed her eyes tightly shut so as not to have to see Bruce astride that bike riding away from her, out of her life. Yet, even though she didn't see him, the picture stayed in her mind all the way home.

"I'll have a glass of wine, since you're pouring."

Aggie stood staring at her friend, and overflowed her own glass. Then, without a word, she got another from the cupboard, filled it, and passed it across the table. Steve dabbed the overflow from around his wife's glass with a napkin, carefully not looking at Mary.

Mary lifted her wineglass in a toast. "To friends," she said. Steve and Aggie murmured appropriately, clicked their glasses against hers, and sipped. The meal proceeded with polite conversation, none of which Mary could even recall.

"Will you have a bit more?" asked Aggie half an hour later, with the dinner nearly finished.

"No, thanks. One's my limit."

"I can see that," said Aggie, handing Mary a fresh napkin. "The one you've had seems to have induced a crying jag."

"I'm not really crying," Mary said, watching the drops soaking into the yellow linen cloth.

"Then why are your eyes leaking?"

"I don't know. They've been doing it a lot lately."

"Bartenderitis, no doubt," Aggie said.

"No doubt," whispered Mary.

Steve got up, excused himself, and wandered into the den, closing the door behind him.

"Okay, talk."

The yellow napkin grew wetter. "It's been two weeks. You told me to give him a bit of time, then try again. I did, but he won't see me. He won't talk to me. He got an answering machine, and he doesn't return my calls. The staff at the pub all know my voice now and have instructions not to call him to the phone. I feel like a . . . groupie. I guess one weekend with me was all he ever wanted. Or he discovered that one weekend with me was enough."

"Do you really believe that?" Aggie asked.

"What else can I believe?"

"That you hurt him badly by telling him you wouldn't have been in his bed unless you'd been so lonely you couldn't help yourself? That in spite of what you shared that weekend, in spite of the closeness you'd developed in the time you'd known each other before that, you still weren't prepared to have a relationship with a bar owner? He is what he is, Mary, and you can't change that."

"I know, and that's what I want to tell him. That I don't care what he does. That if he wants to run a bar, I'll learn to deal with it."

"There is one way," Aggie said. "You could go there and confront him. I mean, how could he refuse to talk to you, to listen to you, if you did it in front of a hundred other people?"

Mary paled. "Go there? How could I? I'd be so embarrassed! All the staff know. . . . Aggie, he was so annoyed with me that night. He carried me out like a sack of potatoes. No. That is the one thing I can't do."

"Right," said Aggie. "So I guess that's it. It's over. Well, the best thing to do is make plans of your own that don't include Bruce Hagendorn. There are plenty of men out there, Mary. You don't need him."

"Hello." Mary came to a halt just inside the doors. The same cloud of blue smoke clung to the ceiling. The nest of sticks and twigs in the corner now had a stuffed raven sitting in it, blue-black feathers gleaming, one bright, golden eye seeming to bore into Mary's mind, enjoying her humiliation. Did dead ravens laugh? "Is Bruce Hagendorn in, please?" She was grateful that at least this was not the waiter who'd served her last time.

"No. No, he doesn't work here anymore. He's probably over at the new place."

New place? He wasn't just part owner of one bar, but two? She swallowed hard. It didn't matter. He could own ninety bars, and she'd still love him. She had to make him see that. "I see. Where is the new place?"

"Oh, it's not open yet."

"That doesn't matter. If he's there, I'd like to go and see him." It would be easier to have this meeting without witnesses.

The young man frowned. "I could call him and ask if it's all right."

Mary felt her hope deflate. She shook her head. "No. Don't bother." There was no point in the man calling to see if it would be all right, because if he knew she was coming, it would *not* be all right.

"Will you let me into Bruce's place, please?" Mary asked the super over her tall stack of Chinese food boxes. "I forgot the key."

Mr. Taylor frowned. "But he's got—Listen, why don't you two just exchange keys and be done with it, then you won't have to keep bothering me all the time."

Over Mr. Taylor's grumbling Commander Riker said, "Warp eight, Mr. Crusher. Destination Starbase . . ."

"Please, Mr. Taylor? This stuff is heavy." To say nothing of hot. The Moo Goo Gai Pan was burning her left wrist.

"All right, all right. But I want the keys back. Both of them."

Both of them? Mary pondered as she elbowed the elevator button, trying to remember if she'd ever gotten a spare key to Bruce's apartment and forgotten to give it back. She didn't think so.

With one arm she cleared enough space in Bruce's cluttered kitchen to put down the food containers. She looked at her watch. It was just ten o'clock. When would he be home? Since the new bar wasn't open, she didn't think he'd be late. Her insides fluttered, and she hoped they'd settle down enough by the time he arrived so that she'd be able to sit and eat calmly while they talked. The Chinese food was to serve as a bribe. She hoped the scent of soy sauce and sesame oil would tempt him into listening, because if she got thrown out, the dinner went with her.

Bruce, she would say, in a calm, reasonable tone, *I love you and I know you love me. We have problems, it is true, but I believe we can work them out. I'm reconciled—*No. Reconciled sounded as if she was accepting what he did in spite of herself, as if she still hated it but was willing to be reasonable if that were what he really wanted and was unable to be reasonable himself and do things her way.

Bruce, we're two adults in love with each other. I'm sure you've made mistakes before in your life. I know I made one two weeks ago, and I'd like a chance to rectify it.

Lord! That sounded like a textbook suggestion for handling conflict! "Get real, Mary," she said aloud, and then looked down at her hands busy cleaning the sink. "Dammit! What am I doing here? Do I want the man to come home and find me smelling like chlorine?" She rinsed the cloth, hung it neatly over the edge of the scoured sink, and angrily wiped down the counter she'd absently cleared off.

Bruce, I love you, and while I'm aware that you've never asked me to marry you, if you ever do, I want you to know that I have no intention of being your galley slave in addition to being your wife.

"Oh, dammit! Get out of the kitchen, idiot. Go sit down in the living room . . . seductively!"

Mary turned off all but one light in the far corner of the room, and set it on its dimmest switch, arranged the full skirt of her red dress artfully on the cushions of Bruce's brown couch, fluffed her hair on her bare shoulders, fixed a smile on her mouth, and tried to relax. She sat rigidly, staring at the door. The hour beeped on the watch he'd left lying on the coffee table. Mary jumped. The silence stretched on. The aroma of Chinese food faded. Mary slumped sideways, head falling onto a pillow while she planned what she would say. She may as well be comfortable while she waited. She'd hear his key in the lock and could sit up, fix her hair, and put her smile back on before he was even aware that she was there.

Bruce, I can't go on with things like this between us. Please let me tell you how much I love you. When I said I was lonely, I was lonely for you. I love you. I need you. I want to be with you no matter what. . . .

The watch beeped again. Mary hardly stirred, just curled her legs up a little closer to her chest, tucked the brown-and-cream checkered pillow under her head, and slept on.

The sound of the door opening woke her, and she sat up, eyes wide, hair tangled in her lashes. She swung her feet to the floor, jumped up, and came out fighting. "Dammit, where have you been?" she demanded, grabbing the front of his filthy sweatshirt. "I've been waiting for hours and hours and the dinner's all cold! How can I make you listen when there isn't even good, hot Chinese food to keep you sitting still while I talk?"

He grabbed her wrists, tore her hands free of his shirt, and bellowed at her, "It's two-thirty in the damned morning! How the hell long have you been here? Do you know how many hours I've spent waiting in your apartment for you, Mary DeLaney? I've paced the rug bare! I've called every hospital in the lower mainland at least twice; the cops think I'm some kind of nut-case, and if it wasn't for the fact that I finally woke Jerry Taylor up and he told me where to find you, I might have spent the rest of the damn night waiting for you and . . . and if you don't kiss me right this minute, I might go even more insane."

She kissed him. Right that minute, and for many more minutes after.

"I love you," she said when she could talk. She was squashed deliciously between his body and the back of the couch. "I sat here for hours thinking up ways to get you to listen to me. I rehearsed all sorts of little speeches, but now that you're here, all I can think of to say is that I love you."

He smiled, catching her finger as she stroked his mustache. He kissed it, then curled it up under the bottom of his sweatshirt. "That's all you ever have to tell me," he said. "All I ever want to know. But I have things to tell you too. Pull."

"Pull?"

"With that finger I put there. I put it there for a reason, you know."

She had to use more than one finger curled under the lower edge of his sweatshirt, but it came off quickly.

"What do you have to tell me that can be more

important than telling me that you love me, which you haven't done yet tonight?"

"Haven't I? I thought I was doing a fairly adequate job of showing you. I love you. And I'm sorry for the things I said."

"Me too. I have to tell you this, Bruce. When I said I was lonely, I meant for you."

"I know that, doll." He smoothed a hand over her shoulder, carrying the thin strap of her red cotton dress with it. His mouth followed. She shivered. "I knew it then but . . ."

"But I'd hurt you, and you were striking out."

"You got it." He lifted his head. "It's going to be strange, married to a shrink. You'll know the reason behind everything I do and say."

She went very still. "Are you going to be married to a shrink?"

He met her gaze soberly. "Only if her name's Mary DeLaney, and only if she says yes."

She smiled. "A shrink is a psychiatrist. I'm a psychologist."

"What's the difference?"

"A degree in medicine and about a hundred and fifty bucks an hour. I'm not hoping to get rich, Bruce."

"What are you hoping for?" he asked against her breast.

"To get loved. Soon," she whispered, tangling her hands in his hair.

"Is that your way of saying yes?"

"Just one of them. I have others."

"Show me," he invited huskily.

Sometime later, he lifted his torso up and looked at her, laughing. "I have never," he said, "made love to a lady in a red dress."

She looked down. "Only half in it. And I have never made love to a man half in dirty jeans."

He finished shucking them with a couple of kicks. "I have never," he went on, "been in such a big hurry before."

He ran a hand down her front, cupping it over her womb. He looked at her seriously. "What if . . ."

"I can't think of anything I'd like better."

She saw him swallow. "Will my baby be as important to you as—I mean, will you love her as much?"

She forced back the stinging tears that rose in the backs of her eyes. She met his gaze with a smile. "Yes," she said. "All our babies will be just as important as Andy was. I will love them as much. How many will you give me?"

"*I* give *you*? Won't it be the other way around? We can have as many as you want, as you're willing to have. Just so long as you give me a blue-eyed daughter."

"I'll do my best." She linked her hands behind his neck as he rolled to his side on the wide sofa. "For a guy who was so dead set against having a wife and babies and a little farm somewhere, you've sure changed your tune, my Stud."

"For a lady who was so dead set against having any kind of relationship with a bar owner, you have too."

She nodded. "I was being pretty stupid about it. About a lot of things. Letting my fears take over. Letting guilt rule me."

"I'm proud of you for overcoming your fears," he said, then rolled off the couch, lifting her with him, staggering as he fought for balance. "But I'm not too happy at being kicked out of the parking space I'd come to think of as my own."

"Is that why you went to my apartment tonight? Why you decided to forgive me?" she asked. "Because you knew I'd bought a car, so I must be growing up at last?"

"It wasn't a case of my forgiving you," he said. "You hadn't done anything so terrible. I had. I came to ask you to forgive me, and to show you this."

He walked to the table by the door and picked up a sheaf of papers, slapping it on his hand as he returned. "I sold out my share of the Raven's Nest," he said. "I don't own a bar anymore. But I do own this."

He handed her the papers. She looked at them, but the words meant nothing to her. "It's a night-club for teens. A dry one, of course. I figure if we catch them young enough, we might be able to teach them that they can have fun without booze or drugs. A very important lady once told me something like that would help. It's out in the suburbs, where lots of kids live."

"Oh." Her eyes were wide and intensely blue as she gazed up at him.

"Upstairs on the other two floors I figured we could maybe have lounges with games and things, and meeting rooms and maybe even a few flops for kids who have no place to go. Will you help me? Can we do it? What do you think?"

"I can't think," she said, stunned. "I can't talk."

He laughed. "Can you nod your head?"

She nodded her head, splashing happy tears all over his chest.

"Can you help me with it?"

Again, she nodded her head.

"Can you think of any other ways to say yes?"

She nuzzled her face against his neck. "That depends on the question."

"Prepare yourself," he said scooping her into his arms and striding into his bedroom. "Because I have lots and lots of those."

To his eternal delight she had all the right answers.

THE EDITOR'S CORNER

It's been a while since we acknowledged and thanked the many people here at Bantam who work so hard to make our LOVESWEPTs the best they can be. Aside from our small editorial staff, members of the art department, managing editorial department, production, sales, and marketing departments, to name a few, all contribute their expertise to the project. The department whose input is most apparent to you, the reader, is that of our art department, so I'd like to mention them briefly this month.

Getting the cover art exactly right isn't an easy task. No two people ever envision the characers the same way—and think of how many people read our books! Our art director, Beverly Leung, knows how important it is for you to have a beautiful cover to look at. Her job starts by commissioning an artist for a particular book. The artist is given a description sheet prepared by the author herself. After models who most closely resemble the characters are selected, a photographic shoot is done, and from those photos the artist/illustrator creates first a sketch and finally a painting for the cover.

During the entire process Beverly works to ensure we—and ultimately you—are pleased with the finished artwork. She's done a fabulous job since taking on the assignment, and it's reflected in the gorgeous covers we're able to bring you. Thanks, Beverly.

Now on to the good stuff! Next month's LOVESWEPTs feature heroes so yummy, anyone on a diet should beware! Kay Hooper weaves another magical web around you with **THROUGH THE LOOKING GLASS,** LOVESWEPT #408, the next in her *Once Upon a Time . . .* series. Financial wizard Gideon Hughes fully intends to shut down the carnival he had inherited. But when he arrives to check it out, he's instantly enchanted by manager Maggie Durant—and balance sheets loose all interest for him. Gideon is intrigued and unnerved by Maggie's forthrightness, but something compels him to explore the deep and strange feelings she stirs in him. Then Maggie openly declares her love for Gideon and in so doing, lays claim to his heart. Amid clowns, gypsies, and magicians, Gideon and the silver-haired siren find the most wondrous love—and together they create their own Wonderland.

In **PRIVATE EYES,** LOVESWEPT #409, Charlotte Hughes delivers the kind of story you ask for most often—one that combines lighthearted humor with powerful emotion. Private investigator Jack Sloan resents being asked to train his
(continued)

partner's niece, Ashley Rogers. He takes one look at her and decides she doesn't belong on an undercover assignment, she belongs in a man's arms—preferably in his. But he soon discovers he's underestimated the lovely single mother of two. Ashley works harder than he ever imagined, and her desire to win his approval tugs at his heart—a heart he thought had long ago gone numb. Charlotte puts these two engaging characters in some hilarious situations—and also in some intimate ones. Don't miss this very entertaining romance!

Sandra Chastain often focuses on people living in small towns, and her knack for capturing the essence of a community and the importance of belonging really makes her books special. In **RUN WILD WITH ME**, LOVESWEPT #410, Sandra brings together a wicked-looking cowboy, and a feisty lady law officer. Andrea Fleming has spent her life in Arcadia, Georgia, and she's convinced it's where she belongs. Her one attempt to break away had ended in heartache and disaster. Sam Farley is a stranger in a town that doesn't take kindly to outsiders. He doesn't understand how someone can have ties to a place—until he falls for Andrea. She makes the handsome wanderer crave what he's never known. This is a touching, emotional love story of two lost people who find their true soul mates.

Deborah Smith's heroes are never lacking in good looks or virility—and the hero of **HONEY AND SMOKE**, LOVESWEPT #411, is no exception. Ex-marine Max Templeton could have walked off the cover of *Soldier of Fortune* magazine. But when he encounters Betty Quint in a dark mountain cave, he finds in her one worthy adversary. Betty is a city girl who has moved back to the town of her ancestors to return to the basics and run a small catering business and restaurant. She can't believe the man beneath the camouflage and khaki is also the local justice of the peace! Of course, there's no peace for her once Max invades her life. But Betty is looking for commitment. She has dreams of marriage and family, and Max runs his wedding chapel as if it's all in fun—and with the knowledge that marriage is definitely not for him. You'll love being along for the ride as Betty convinces Max to believe in a perfect future, and Max proves to Betty that Rambo has a heart!

Doris Parmett has a lot of fun inventing her wonderful heroes and heroines and researching her stories. For her latest book she visited a local cable television station and had a great time. She was asked to appear on a talk show,
(continued)

and it went so well, they invited her back. Absorbing as much atmosphere and information as she could, Doris returned to work and created the love story we'll bring you next month. In **OFF LIMITS**, LOVESWEPT #412, Joe Michaels and Liz Davis make television screens melt with their weekly hit show. But off camera, Liz fights to keep things all business. Joe refuses to deny the sexual tension that sizzles between them and vows to prove to the vulnerable woman behind the glamorous image that a man can be trusted, that their life together would be no soap opera. These two characters produce a whirlwind of passionate emotion that sweeps the reader along!

What woman hasn't fantasized about being pursued by a ruggedly gorgeous man? Well, in **BLUE DALTON**, LOVESWEPT #413 by Glenna McReynolds, our heroine, Blue, finds the experience exhausting when tracker Walker Evans stalks her into the Rockies. Blue is after the treasure she believes her father left to her alone, and Walker thinks his is the valid claim. When Walker captures her, she can't help but succumb to wild sensation and has no choice but to share the search. Confused by the strength of her desire for Walker, she tries to outsmart him—but her plan backfires along with her vow not to love him. Only Glenna can blend exciting elements of adventure so successfully with the poignant and heartfelt elements that make a story a true romance. Don't miss this unique book!

We're pleased and proud to feature a devoted LOVESWEPT reader from down under as our Fan of the Month for June. Isn't it wonderful to know stories of love and romance are treasured and enjoyed throughout the world!

Hope your summer is filled with great reading pleasures.
Sincerely,

Susann Brailey

Susann Brailey
Editor
LOVESWEPT
Bantam Books
666 Fifth Avenue
New York, NY 10103

FAN OF THE MONTH

Wilma Stubbs

It gives me great pleasure to represent the Australian fans of the LOVESWEPT series, and there are many as evidenced by the fact that one has to be early to get titles by favorite authors such as Kay Hooper, Barbara Boswell, etc.

I have been reading LOVESWEPTs since early 1984 when the Australian publisher distributed a booklet comprised of excerpts from the first titles. I was hooked—and impatient! So I wrote a plaintive letter to New York for a publication date, and the nice people there sent back a letter full of information.

As the mother of two semi-adults with their associated interests and friends, and the wife of a man who has worked shift work for twenty-five years, I've always found romantic fiction to be my favorite retreat. LOVESWEPTs cover a broad range of moods—from the sensuousness of Sandra Brown to the humor of Billie Green to the depth of Mary Kay McComas to the imaginativeness of Iris Johansen, particularly her Clanad series with the delightful touch of mystique.

I have often recommended to troubled friends that they read some of the above authors in order to gain a balance to their lives. It seems to refresh one's spirits to dip into other lives and gain a better perspective on one's own.

60 Minutes to a Better, More Beautiful You!

N ow it's easier than ever to awaken your
sensuality, stay slim forever—even make
yourself irresistible. With Bantam's bestselling
subliminal audio tapes, you're only 60 minutes
away from a better, more beautiful you!

__	45004-2	**Slim Forever**	$8.95
__	45112-X	**Awaken Your Sensuality**	$7.95
__	45035-2	**Stop Smoking Forever**	$8.95
__	45130-8	**Develop Your Intuition**	$7.95
__	45022-0	**Positively Change Your Life**	$8.95
__	45154-5	**Get What You Want**	$7.95
__	45041-7	**Stress Free Forever**	$8.95
__	45106-5	**Get a Good Night's Sleep**	$7.95
__	45094-8	**Improve Your Concentration**	$7.95
__	45172-3	**Develop A Perfect Memory**	$8.95

Bantam Books, Dept. LT, 414 East Golf Road, Des Plaines, IL 60016

Please send me the items I have checked above. I am enclosing $_____
(please add $2.00 to cover postage and handling). Send check or money
order, no cash or C.O.D.s please. (Tape offer good in USA only.)

Mr/Ms _____

Address _____

City/State _____ Zip _____

LT-5/90

Please allow four to six weeks for delivery.
Prices and availability subject to change without notice.

THE LATEST IN BOOKS
AND AUDIO CASSETTES

Paperbacks

☐	27032	**FIRST BORN** Doris Mortman	$4.95
☐	27283	**BRAZEN VIRTUE** Nora Roberts	$3.95
☐	25891	**THE TWO MRS. GRENVILLES** Dominick Dunne	$4.95
☐	27891	**PEOPLE LIKE US** Dominick Dunne	$4.95
☐	27260	**WILD SWAN** Celeste De Blasis	$4.95
☐	25692	**SWAN'S CHANCE** Celeste De Blasis	$4.50
☐	26543	**ACT OF WILL** Barbara Taylor Bradford	$5.95
☐	27790	**A WOMAN OF SUBSTANCE** Barbara Taylor Bradford	$5.95

Audio

☐ **THE SHELL SEEKERS** by Rosamunde Pilcher
Performance by Lynn Redgrave
180 Mins. Double Cassette   48183-9 $14.95

☐ **COLD SASSY TREE** by Olive Ann Burns
Performance by Richard Thomas
180 Mins. Double Cassette   45166-9 $14.95

☐ **PEOPLE LIKE US** by Dominick Dunne
Performance by Len Cariou
180 Mins. Double Cassette   45164-2 $14.95

☐ **CAT'S EYE** by Margaret Atwood
Performance by Kate Nelligan
180 Mins. Double Cassette   45203-7 $14.95

Bantam Books, Dept. FBS, 414 East Golf Road, Des Plaines, IL 60016

Please send me the items I have checked above. I am enclosing $_____
(please add $2.00 to cover postage and handling). Send check or money
order, no cash or C.O.D.s please. (Tape offer good in USA only.)

Mr/Ms _____

Address _____

City/State _____ Zip _____

FBS—4/90

Please allow four to six weeks for delivery.
Prices and availability subject to change without notice.